HENRY THE HOMEMAKER

Henry tried to slip the spatula under the nearest chop. It wouldn't go in, at any angle. The chop appeared to be solidly welded to the pan. He went to the pantry and got his father's hammer and screwdriver. Henry placed the tip of the screwdriver between the chop and the skillet. He hit the end of the screwdriver with the hammer. Hard. The chop rocketed up into the air and sailed across the kitchen to the floor in front of the sink. Joe bent down and picked it up. He dropped it into the sink.

"What'll we do?" Joe whispered.

Henry was busy positioning the screwdriver again. "Wash it off."

"Wash it?"

"Wash it. That's dinner."

Bantam Skylark Books of Related Interest
Ask your bookseller for the books you have missed

Help! There's a Cat Washing in Here!

by Alison Smith

illustrated by Amy Rowen

A Bantam Skylark Book®
Toronto · New York · London · Sydney

RL 5, 008-012

HELP! THERE'S A CAT WASHING IN HERE!
*A Bantam Book / published by arrangement with
E. P. Dutton Inc.*

PRINTING HISTORY
Dutton edition published May 1981
Bantam edition / June 1983

ISBN 0-553-15199-1

Published simultaneously in the United States and Canada

---

*Bantam Books are published by Bantam Books, Inc. Its trade-
mark, consisting of the words "Bantam Books" and the por-
trayal of a rooster, is Registered in U.S. Patent and Trademark
Office and in other countries. Marca Registrada. Bantam
Books, Inc., 666 Fifth Avenue, New York, New York 10103.*

PRINTED IN THE UNITED STATES OF AMERICA

CW   0 9 8 7 6 5 4 3 2 1

to David and Jenny

Chapter One

Tuesday   June 1

HENRY WALKER eased on up to the third step. Now he could see his mother sitting at the dining room table, surrounded by bills and books and bank statements. He clamped his chin down even more tightly on the box of chocolate chip cookies he'd borrowed from the kitchen. Two books began to slip out from under his left elbow. He pressed his arm in on them harder.

He was moving on up to the fourth step now. If his mother looked up and saw him heading up to bed at eleven-thirty, she'd be really angry. But once you were into a television movie where whole cities were being destroyed, and swarms of things and tidal waves were sweeping across the earth, it was hard to just get up and walk away from it. Even when you had figured out how it was all going to end, you wanted to stick with it and watch the state of Rhode Island fall into a crack in the earth.

1

His sneakers, dangling by their laces from his right arm, made carrying his glass of milk tricky—but so far, so good—no spilling. He'd be out of the danger zone, where his mother could see him if she looked up, in another minute. He moved on up to the fifth step very quietly, without taking his eyes off his mother, and set his foot down on the round, wooden handle of Annie's jump rope. He felt his foot rolling, and he dropped everything he was carrying and clutched at space. His body tilted, and he lost his balance and toppled out of control. The hallway flashed past him backwards as he plummeted down the stairs and thudded hard onto the hall floor. He found it impossible to breathe for a moment—and that frightened him even more than falling downstairs had.

It seemed like an hour and a half—or forever—but he knew it was really only a few seconds later when his lungs started to work again. Henry calmed down. At least he knew he was going to live. Ah, yes. There was Annie's jump rope, twined in between and around his legs. There were the things he'd been carrying—spread all across the hall. Unfortunately, the glass of milk had emptied into the cookie box, which would certainly make the mopping up easier, but meant that the cookies were turning to mush in the box, right

before his eyes. And there was his mother. She was standing beside him, looking alarmed.

He said, "Hey, Ma." Two consecutive words were about all he could handle right now.

"Are you all right, Henry?"

"Don't know."

"Well, move something, dear."

Henry moved. Instantly, he was in a lot of pain. Particularly where he'd landed, but also all over. Even the top of his head thumped and ached.

He took a deep, deep breath. When he got his hands on her, that Annie was going to be in pain. How many times had they all told that little monster to clear her junk off those stairs? Even when she actually moved some of it on up to her room, she'd start stacking up a new pile the very next day. The new pile would grow . . . and grow . . . and grow . . . and spread up and down the stairs like one of those creeping blobs from outer space.

"You didn't break anything, did you, dear?"

"Not yet," he said grimly, "but when I get hold of Annie . . ."

His mother reached down and helped him to his feet. "I thought you'd gone to bed hours ago."

"I didn't realize how late it was."

"With a grandfather's clock and a chiming mantel clock in the same room with you, you didn't realize how late it was?"

"Actually, I wasn't too sleepy. You know how it is, Ma."

"Yes, I know how it is. I know that you're supposed to go to bed every single school night at nine-thirty because you have to get up so early." She shook her head. "Honestly, Henry—eleven-thirty."

"Maybe I'd better clean up some of this mess, Ma."

"Maybe you'd better. And when you're through with that, you might just as well come along into the dining room. There's something I have to tell you."

His mother was waiting for him at the dining room table. She held out a fan of papers in her right hand.

"I've been working all night on these bills and on the bank statement, and I have just about come to the end of my rope. In the three years since your father died, we've gone through an awful lot of money. Too much. And now Mr. Toomey, the carpenter, tells me that the house needs a whole new roof before the bad weather comes again in the fall. We're going to have to *do* something. Soon."

"What do you want us to do, Ma? If we need more money, maybe I could get a job after school or whenever."

"Thank you, Henry, but no matter how hard you worked, it wouldn't be enough. Not at your age."

Henry knew she was right. What could he do, anyway? A paper route? . . . mowing lawns, if he could find any to mow? When you were twelve, you could only earn so much.

His mother continued. "There are two possibilities. The first is to sell this house. I know we all love it, but it's so big. Maybe we could find something a lot smaller and cheaper, that we could learn to love in time."

Henry said, "Don't sell the house, Ma. Let's do whatever that second possibility is, instead." The house was big and old. It had about twelve rooms. Three of them were bathrooms, which could come in awfully handy sometimes, like when everyone had the flu. And there were a bunch of little rooms that no one needed, so anybody could use them. There was always plenty of space inside the house for everyone and their friends . . . but when you wanted to be alone, you could have that, too. Henry had always lived there. It was a run-down old house, but he felt very strongly that he did not want to live somewhere else.

His mother said, "Well, if we decided to stay here, I would have to get a job. If I could make some money and nothing else went wrong, we'd manage. If I can't get a job, maybe we could ask Aunt Wilhemina if she'd like to come and live with us. She could pay a little—which would help us—and it would be a saving for her, too.

"Not Aunt Wilhemina!" Henry clapped his hand to his head. Spots appeared before his eyes. He sank back into his chair and groaned out loud.

Aunt Wilhemina ordered people around all day long and expected every kid within earshot—which Henry figured was about three miles if the wind was right—to hop to it, on the double. If you answered her in a normal voice, she'd boom out "I can't *hear* you," and you'd have to boom right back at her—even if it was a very personal and private matter.

Henry felt light-headed. He said, "Hold it right there, Ma," and stumbled out to the kitchen and poured himself a tall glass of milk.

When he came back, his mother said, "Look, Henry, I know Aunt Wilhemina's a little domineering, but no one's perfect. We could set up ground rules and have everything understood before she even moved in. I'm sure, if we tried, we could make it work. And she's always at such loose ends, Henry—with no one to do for. Here, she could help out a little around the house, which would be a real blessing for all of us, particularly if I was working."

Henry took a deep breath. "I'll help out a little. We don't need Aunt Wilhemina. You pick out a good job, and we'll do what we can. We'll eat beans a lot and turn off all the lights and give up desserts. Right there, I bet we can probably save a bundle."

His mother smiled. "I'll give it some thought, Henry. And tomorrow I'll look at the want ads. But even if I agree to try it your way, you'll have to understand that if it doesn't seem to be working out, we'll have to go right on to one of the other possibilities before we get in too deep. And it will mean everyone having to help with things like the laundry and cooking and cleaning."

"I know that."

"There may be more to keeping a family going than you realize. Joe is only ten. And Annie's only six. So you would have to do a lot of the work yourself." She paused. "I don't know how to say this without hurting your feelings, dear, but housekeeping has never been one of your strong points."

"I know that, Ma. But this is different."

"Some weeks, it's all I can do to get you to collect your own dirty laundry and just bring it downstairs, let alone do anyone else's."

"Right. But I don't want to move. I really like this old place."

"And if I ask you to pour your own orange juice in the mornings, you get huffy."

"Not always. Did you know that we all get along better than any family I know, Ma? . . . Just the four of us. But the minute Aunt Wilhemina shows up, it's 'Do this,' and 'Do that,' and in five minutes we're all snapping at each other. Haven't you noticed that?"

"That may be because she doesn't let you get away with as much as I do," his mother said thoughtfully.

"Whatever. The point is, she likes things one way, and we like them another. So let's not spoil a good thing."

"The point is, you're saying you'll take care of everything, but in the past you have never shown the slightest willingness . . ."

"I'm willing, now."

". . . or ability to help out at home."

"Ma—how much ability can it take—to stuff clothes into a washing machine?"

"Thank you, Henry."

"I'm sorry, Ma. You know what I mean."

"Well, maybe it's worth a try, since you seem so determined. And I'm sure Joe and Annie will do what they can to help, *if* you approach them the right way."

Henry smiled a broad smile of anticipation and

said, "Annie can start with those stairs. She can start with them tomorrow." He looked up at the clock. Five past twelve. It was tomorrow, already.

Chapter Two

Wednesday   June 2

As HENRY WOKE UP, all the spots he'd landed on, coming down the stairs the night before, began to throb, or ache, or pound with pain, according to how hard he'd landed on them. He got dressed very slowly and limped downstairs to find Annie. He had something to say to her.

He found her in the kitchen. She was sitting on the floor, struggling to stuff her foot into a beaded moccasin she'd worn when she was still in diapers. Her face was turning red from the effort.

"I nearly broke my neck last night, Annie, falling over your red jump rope. It was lying on the stairs, as usual. Things have got to change around here. You've got to change."

She turned and squinted up at him. "How could you fall over my jump rope if it was just lying on the stairs?"

Henry gritted his teeth. "Never mind *how* it happened. It shouldn't have been on the stairs. I could have killed myself."

"Well, I was going to take it up," Annie said reasonably. "You didn't hurt that rope, did you, Henry? That's the best rope I ever had."

"Your rope is just fine, but I—your own brother—am standing here in deep pain. Annie—are you listening to me?" He tapped her on the top of her smooth, hard head. "I ought to wrap that rope around your neck. If you ever . . ."

"Henry," his mother said, in a warning tone of voice. She was turning pancakes at the stove.

Annie stood up and went over to her mother. "Henry is always picking on me, mother dear. I love you."

"Picking on you? Picking on you! I'm in agony all over because you left your stuff on the stairs, and I'm picking on you?"

Joe came into the kitchen and started piling pancakes, three at a time, onto a plate. "You fell down the stairs, again?"

"Yes, I fell down the stairs again. The monster left a lot of her stuff piled on the stairs, and I didn't see it. And you eat too much!"

"But she's always doing that. Why don't you just watch where you're going?" Joe carried his plate over to the table and sat down.

Henry closed his eyes briefly. This family was

driving him crazy. How was he ever going to turn those two into an efficient housekeeping team?

As if she'd been reading his mind, his mother touched his arm and said, "After breakfast, I want to show you an ad I found in the morning paper. It's almost too good to be true. It sounds perfect for me. And I've told Joe and Annie about our problem, and they both said they'd help."

This was not the time to admit that he was having his doubts about Joe and Annie. Particularly Annie. He said, "Right, Ma," and picked up a plate.

The ad said:

ILLUSTRATOR—child. bks.—exper.
Work at home or with estab. design studio in
S. Hutton. Call Mr. Bennett 555–2000

Henry said, "Are you experienced, Ma?"

"Yes, I am. Well, at least I was. That's just what I did before I got married, when I worked with Rainbow House. I illustrated children's books."

"Have you called this Mr. Bennett?"

"Not yet." She sat down, clutching the paper.

"So, call now."

"Oh, no. Not now. It's way too early. He might not be in. The switchboard might not even be open."

13

"Then no one will answer—or someone will say, 'He's not in.'"

His mother nodded. But she stayed sitting down.

Henry stood up. "Look, Ma—do you want someone else to get that job?"

"No. I'll call."

Henry noticed that her hands, resting on the newspaper, were trembling. It amazed and astonished him that his mother, who he admired so much, was having trouble finding the courage to call this Mr. Bennett, who was just a name in an ad. If it had been up to him, he'd have tackled a hundred Mr. Bennetts rather than voluntarily ask Aunt Wilhemina to move in and take over.

He said, "Ma—"

She jumped. "Yes?"

"Good luck. I hope you get it. I know you're going to get it."

"I don't know, Henry." Her voice was quavery. "All of a sudden, it seems like so long ago that I had to go in for job interviews, or worked outside the house, or even just painted for my own pleasure."

Henry did some arithmetic in his head. "Well, it was about thirteen years ago. I guess that is a long time."

Right away, he could see that this bit of information hadn't made her feel better. He said, "Good luck, Ma," and left, before he could say something that would make her even more upset.

What with experiencing severe pain every time he had to sit down, and an unexpected math test (study history all night long, Henry thought, and they'll spring a math test on you every time), *and* the theft of his lunch (he found it, later, on top of all the stuff in a trash can, looked through it, and put it back in the can and ordered hot lunch, or "ptomaine tuna," as his friends called it), Henry didn't have too much time to wonder how his mother was getting along with Mr. Bennett. But the minute he came through the front door, he called, "Ma—are you home? How'd it go?"

She came down the hall, smiling and breathless.

Henry said, "You got it!"

"No. Not yet. But Mr. Bennett looked at my portfolio of work from Rainbow House, and he liked it! He said if I would do a new portfolio, using a more contemporary approach, he'd probably hire me."

"How big a job is that—doing a new portfolio?"

"Tremendous."

"How long did he give you?"

"Two weeks. I go back to see him on the sixteenth. That's as long as he can wait for me."

"Is two weeks long enough?"

"Not nearly. But this is such a big chance, Henry. If I can do it, we'll be all set. I can work right here at home, and we won't have to sell the house—or invite Aunt Wilhemina to come and live with us. And I want to do it. It was so exciting, being back in an office like that and seeing all the work in progress. I want to do it."

Henry couldn't remember when he'd seen her so excited about anything. A small, sharp twinge of jealousy shot through his midsection. Then, when he remembered what the money would mean, he felt better.

His mother took his arm and led him into the living room. "That's what I need to talk to you about now, Henry. I'll need to have things quiet for the next two weeks. No distractions at all. First, I'll go up to Boston for a day, to buy some materials. Then after that, I'll set up all my things in the attic room, and you and Joe and Annie will have to keep the house, and yourselves, going—and be really quiet. Being the oldest, you'll have to take on a lot of the responsibility for the whole family."

"Right."

"Are you *sure* you can handle this, Henry—and keep up your grades and get enough sleep?" She studied him for a minute and shook her head. "I could still call Aunt Wilhemina. She'd be over first thing in the morning. I know she would. And we could just invite her for the next two weeks . . . to see how it worked out."

"No!" Henry suddenly remembered a story he'd heard once about an Arab who'd let his camel stick his nose into the Arab's tent, and then his head and shoulders—and then his whole front half. In no time at all, the Arab had found himself on the outside of the tent, looking in at the camel who'd taken over inside. "We'll be just fine. I can do it, Ma. Really."

His mother had already gone out to stand on the corner and wait for the Boston bus when Henry came downstairs Thursday morning. He'd overslept a little, being accustomed to having her wake him a second time after he'd turned his alarm off and gone back to sleep. There was a note for Henry propped up on the kitchen table.

Make sure Annie remembers her lunch. She'll need a nickel for milk. The cereal's on top of the refrigerator. Don't let Annie pour her own or help herself to the sugar. You do it. Tell Joe he is not to take Throckmorton to school in his lunch box or his pocket. If he does, I'll make him let Throckmorton go when I get home. And this time, I mean it!

Love,
Ma

Henry got out the white bread, mayonnaise and bologna, and cleared a space on the counter by shoving the cookbooks, mixing bowls, flower seed packets and blender to one side, with the flat of his arm. He dealt out six pieces of white bread like a card shark—fast and smooth. He plunged a spatula into the mayonnaise and with one sweeping motion down the counter had applied mayonnaise to all six pieces of bread—and a lot of the counter. He flipped out the slabs of bologna, skimming them through the air like small pink Frisbees to land precisely on the slices of bread. This whole cooking business was probably a breeze, once you tackled it the right way, he thought. Women made too much out of it, altogether. He finished off by dealing out six more slices of bread—*slap, slap, slap*—and sliding each sandwich into a sandwich bag. Two minutes flat, and he'd made all the lunches. While he was rummaging around in the kitchen drawers trying to find lunch bags, Annie and Joe came down and started to whine at him about breakfast.

"Get the cereal down," he told Joe, "—and the milk's in the refrigerator. Can't you two do anything for yourselves?"

He finally found a large grocery bag which he cut in half and folded over and over to fit Annie's sandwich. Then he found a weird bag that had

come from the stationery store and put his own sandwiches in that. Because it was so long and skinny, he had to sort of bend his sandwiches to get them in, but he was running late now, and had no more time to waste on bags. Joe always took his three sandwiches in his lunch box.

He ran upstairs for Annie's nickel—her teacher hated to make change, so a dime, or a quarter, wouldn't do—and came down just in time to hear the front door slam. The school bus must be coming! He skidded into the kitchen, grabbed his own lunch, and sprinted for the bus. He made it, just as the yellow doors started to creak shut. He slipped Annie her nickel for milk and sank into a seat, exhausted. He was glad to have his first morning of being in charge behind him.

His stomach rumbled and cramped a little. Henry sat upright again. With all the excitement, he'd forgotten to eat his own breakfast. Now, even his stomach hurt. What a life!

By ten o'clock, he was so hungry his stomach was making strange noises, which were causing the kids around him to turn and stare at him. He opened his lunch bag as quietly as possible in his lap, and then he dropped his pen as loudly as possible. While he bent down to pick up his pen, he took several large bites out of one sandwich. From then on, every five minutes or so, he'd drop the pen again and eat some more, till Mrs. McClintock said, "Henry, if you can't hang onto your things, maybe you'd better come up and leave them on my desk till the end of class."

Of course, everyone thought that was very funny—particularly the kids who were sitting around Henry's desk. Henry nearly choked on the bite he had in his mouth, trying to get it down fast so he could answer her.

"I'm sorry, Mrs. McClintock. Nothing else will drop."

"I certainly hope not."

He ate the rest of his lunch on the way to his next class. And without milk, it wasn't easy.

Joe sat down beside him on the school bus going home. "I got a note from my teacher. You want to sign it?"

"Why should I sign it?"

"Because Ma's gone to Boston, and when she's away, you're sort of in charge, aren't you?"

"Ma will be back before supper. What'd you do?"

Joe shrugged. "Nothing, really. She's just always getting upset about every little thing." He handed Henry a much folded square of paper.

Henry unfolded the note.

Dear Mrs. Walker,

  I understood, or thought I understood, at our last meeting, that your son Joseph would not be bringing his frog, Throckmorton, to school anymore. I regret to inform you that this time he has gone too far, and it will be necessary for you to discuss this matter with our principal, Mr. Steere. Joseph is excused from further class attendance until such a discussion has taken place.

Thank you.

Mrs. Regina Reilly

Chapter Three

Thursday   June 3

HENRY SAID, "You took Throckmorton to school? After Ma said never again?" He remembered his mother's morning note and winced. "You've really done it this time, Joe. You've gotten yourself and that stupid frog and me into a lot of trouble."

Joe said, "He's not so stupid."

"Well, you are then. There's no way we can keep this from Ma."

"Couldn't you sign it for her—and put on it that

you're too busy to talk to Mr. Steere right now, but that you'll drop by first chance you get?"

"That's forgery. You can go to jail for that, fool."

"I don't want to go to jail over a frog."

"If you ever take that frog to school again"—Henry searched for just the right threat—"I'll burn up every one of your comics in the incinerator."

"Ma wouldn't let you."

"Listen, once Ma's read that note, she'll probably help me."

Henry folded the note and put it in his pocket. "You keep your mouth shut and let me handle this. OK?"

Joe nodded.

His mother was standing in the kitchen when Henry walked in. Her arms were still full of packages, and her purse hung from one wrist. She was staring at the kitchen table.

"Hi, Ma. How'd it go? When did you get home?"

"Just now. The bus dropped me off. What happened here?"

Henry looked at the table. A small hill of sugar and a large puddle of milk had combined to form a solid mound of melted gray sugar beside Annie's bowl, which still contained a lot of soggy cereal

23

flakes. Several half-empty glasses of milk, an open box of cereal, and a half-dozen dirty spoons surrounded the empty sugar bowl.

"We got up a little late."

His mother nodded and pointed at the counter. The bologna he'd left out on the counter had turned an ugly brick red and was curling up at the edges, as were the top slices of the stale loaf of bread he'd left open beside it. The mayonnaise in the mayonnaise jar was either transparent, like melted fat—or all thick and yellow, like custard.

Henry said, "I had a little trouble finding the lunch bags."

"Henry, I know you probably tried, but this"—she waved her hand at the table—"this is a mess."

"I know, Ma. But all I need to do is work out a system, see? When I've got it all figured out, with everyone doing something here and there, it'll all be done in no time—maybe an hour a day. I just need time, Ma."

His mother sighed. "I think I'll go upstairs and have a nice, hot bath."

"That's a great idea. You do that." Henry waited till the kitchen door had closed behind her, and then he went to work. He grabbed the bologna, bread, and mayonnaise and dumped them into the trash. Then he started on the table. It took several minutes of picking and hacking with a blunt knife to get all the solidified sugar up off the table.

Henry worked fast. He wanted the kitchen to look . . . well, at least normal, by the time his mother came back downstairs for her stuff. There was still that little matter of the note about Joe and Throckmorton.

For supper, Annie set the table. Everyone got forks, but not everyone got a knife . . . and there was some heated discussion about where the spoons went, until Henry threatened to stick one in her ear if she didn't put them on the right side of each plate. Joe was in charge of the hot dog rolls and the relishes. Henry heated up the hot dogs. It wasn't fancy eating, but there was a lot of it. Henry had heated up two pounds of hot dogs.

When everyone was pleasantly stuffed, Henry cleared his throat and said, casually, "Mrs. Reilly wants you to call Mr. Steere tomorrow morning, Ma. Just for a minute."

"About what?"

"About Joe . . . and Throckmorton."

"Henry! Didn't you even read that note I left you? I expressly said that Joe wasn't to take that frog to school."

"I know, Ma. I read the note, honest. But I was so busy—you remember that I said we got up a little late?—that I just forgot to frisk him."

His mother turned on Joe. "And you! I've

25

warned you. This is the last straw. How many times have I told you . . . ?"

Annie leaned forward and asked, "Where'd you put him this time?"

"He was sitting in her big drawer when she came back after lunch. He hopped right out, into her lap."

Annie persisted. "What'd she do, Joey? Did she scream?"

"Did she ever! Mr. Steere came all the way down the hall to see what had happened."

"Did everyone laugh?"

Joe nodded. "Michael Toohey fell off his chair, he laughed so hard." He grinned. "She made me and Michael stay in at recess."

His mother said, "Joe—you're going to have to let Throckmorton go."

Joe said, "Please don't make me let him go now, Ma. He's so little. Later on, maybe, in the middle of the summer I'll let him go. I promise. Not now. I won't do it again. And all I did was keep him in my lunch box. Michael Toohey was the one who took him out and put him in her drawer. I didn't do that, Ma."

Henry said, "I'll frisk him every morning, Ma. Swear to God. It won't happen again."

Annie said, "Please let him keep dear Throckmorton, dear mummy. He's so sweet and green, like a pickle," and she started to giggle. "Throckmorton P. Pickle. I shall call him Mr. Pickle from now on."

Henry's mother sighed. "All right. He gets one more chance. It'll be your responsibility, Henry—because obviously I cannot rely on Joe—to see that the frog stays here."

"Yes, ma'am."

She looked at them all and sighed again and shook her head. "We haven't exactly gotten off to a flying start with this new program, Henry."

Henry also sighed. When she was right, she was right.

Chapter Four

Friday   June 4

AROUND TWO IN THE MORNING, Henry woke up hungry. He fought the feeling for a while, but it was no use. He'd have to go downstairs and get something to make his stomach comfortable, or he'd be awake all night.

His mother was seated at the kitchen table, fully dressed.

"Are you still up?" he asked. "Haven't you gone to bed at all, yet?"

"No. I wanted to get everything fixed up in the attic—so I could get started bright and early to-morrow. I mean today."

"Is it the way you want it now?"

"I think so. The big skylight makes the lighting perfect, and there's plenty of space." She shook her head. "I certainly won't be able to say that I didn't have a good work area."

Henry poured himself a glass of milk. "Then you're all set, right?"

There was a long silence. "I don't know. I have an awful lot to learn. Things have really changed. And I've forgotten a lot, too."

"It'll come back to you. Won't it?"

"I hope so."

"Sure it will."

"Sometimes, I feel so excited . . . so charged up, that it's sort of hard to settle down to work, and even that scares me a little. What if I never do manage to settle down? Do you know what I mean?"

Henry frowned. "Not really. But you will. Settle down."

"Well," she said, standing up, "good night."

"Good night."

When his alarm went off Friday morning, Henry sat up immediately, tingling unpleasantly with anxiety. He'd been dreaming that Aunt Wilhemina had banished him to a life outside of their house. "You can look in through the windows all you like," she'd said, "but you may not come in ever again." When he'd stood outside a window, begging her to allow him back into the family, she'd just smiled cheerfully at him from inside the house and shouted, "I can't *hear* you!" over and over. Henry felt a damp chill where the bedroom air touched his sweating neck. Boy! Even at a distance, Aunt Wilhemina could drive him crazy.

He'd expected to be the first one downstairs, but his mother's breakfast dishes were already rinsed and stacked in the sink, and there was another note on the table.

Dear Henry,
    Remember, I am relying on you to keep Throckmorton and Joe out of any more trouble. I'll call the school at eight. Annie will need a nickel, and make her wear her rubbers—it's raining. Since we are all out of sugar, everyone will have to have eggs this morning—or cereal without sugar.

Love,
Ma

P. S. Clean up!

Joe came down in a bad mood, barely answering when Henry relayed the contents of the note. Henry offered to make a panful of scrambled eggs for all of them, and when Joe didn't answer, he took this as a sign that he should go ahead. He'd seen his mother scramble eggs a thousand times. He heated the skillet, threw in some butter, and turned towards the toaster to start making the breakfast toast. He had just finished the first four slices when he noticed the blue gray smoke in the air around his head. The butter! The pan was glowing dully where it rested on the burner, and there was a cone of dense smoke billowing up out of it as the butter burned. Henry grabbed the pan to pull it off the burner, and dropped it with a howl of pain. Even the handle was hot enough to blister. Burnt butter splattered all over the kitchen floor, and the smell of burning linoleum rose to mingle with the smell of scorched butter.

"Wow!" Joe said reverently.

"Get the paper towels!" Henry snapped.

He found a pot holder and picked up the skillet. A smoking, dark brown circle showed where it had rested on the linoleum. Joe said, "Wow!" again. Henry grabbed the paper towels from him and mopped up the floor.

"Get out the cereal."

"No eggs? Ma said we could have eggs."

"No eggs. Cereal."

"But there's no sugar," Joe said. "I can't eat that stuff without sugar."

"You want it sweet? Here! I'll sweeten it for you." Henry poured a cupful of cereal into a bowl, snatched the maple syrup from the cabinet, and dribbled maple syrup all over the cereal. "Now, it's sweet. Eat it!"

Obediently, Joe sat down. He dipped a spoon into the mixture and laid a little on the tip of his tongue. A smile appeared on his face. "It's great. I like it. Hey—this is better than sugar."

"Fine." Henry started on the lunches.

Annie walked in, sniffing the air like a short, fat bloodhound. "This kitchen smells funny."

Henry ignored that. "Joe will pour you some cereal. I'm putting a nickel in your lunch bag, and wear your rubbers."

"All right, dear Henry. I shall wear my rubbers." She turned to Joe. "And how is Mr. Throckmorton Pickle, this morning?"

Joe looked at her suspiciously. "Fine."

Henry said, "Put some syrup on that cereal for her, Joe."

"Thank you, dear Henry. Thank you, dear Joseph."

Joe said, "She's up to something."

Henry sighed. "I know it. What's up, Annie?"

Annie bent over her cereal bowl and jammed a very large spoonful of cereal into her mouth.

Then she looked up at Henry and pointed to her bulging cheeks.

"She can't talk. Her mouth is full," Henry said.

"She looks like a hamster," Joe said. He got up and started to collect his school things.

"Wait a minute," Henry said. "Empty your pockets."

Joe pulled out the linings of his pockets. No sign of a frog. Henry checked his lunch box. It was frog-free. "Where's Throckmorton?"

"He's upstairs, in his cage."

"He'd better be. By the time you get into class, Ma will probably have talked to Mr. Steere—but if there's any problem, tell them she's going to call first chance she gets this morning."

"Right. I'm going into the living room and watch TV till it's time to go."

"You go down to the bus stop and watch the traffic go by till it's time to go. Last time you went into the living room to watch the TV, you missed the bus."

"It's raining! I'm not going to stand down there in the rain."

"Stand under a tree."

"I'm going to tell Ma."

"You even try to tell Ma, and I'm going to *try* to break your leg."

Joe left, slamming the front door so loudly the windows rattled. Henry hoped his mother hadn't heard it, but he knew that the people living three houses down had probably heard it. He sighed and turned his attention to locating Annie's rubbers. He wondered again what Annie was up to. She put on her own rubbers without any argument and headed for the bus stop, singing some weird, sick little song about eating frogs who looked too much like sweet, sweet pickles. He shook his head. Any time the kid was that happy, it was something really big.

His mother had done some food shopping before Henry got home. There were two large cans of green beans and a box of instant potatoes on the counter, and another note.

Dear Henry,
   Tonight, we're having a slightly more balanced meal—green beans, mashed potatoes, and hamburgers. You'll find the meat in the refrigerator. I'll do the dishes. This morning must have gone better—except for the linoleum, of course. Is Annie up to something? Her room was neat this morning.

Love,
Ma.

Henry shook his head. He'd planned to heat up a couple of cans of vegetable soup and serve it with cut-up, leftover hot dogs floating around in it. Period. If his mother expected a lot of fancy cooking from him, he was going to need a lot more help in the kitchen.

When he came downstairs to tackle the hamburgers at five-thirty, Annie had already set the table. Each place had a knife, a fork, and a spoon . . . but they were all on the left side. Well, the kid was trying. Each place had a glass, a plate, and a paper napkin. You had to give her credit. And there were five places set. So, her counting was a little off. Henry collected the extra silverware and dish, and put them away.

He had his head stuck in the refrigerator, looking for the hamburger, when he heard the front door slam and the rise and fall of two girl-sounding voices. He shut the refrigerator door and went out to the front hall. Annie was helping a small, dark-haired girl hang up her raincoat. The new kid had a suitcase clutched in her free hand. She stared at Henry.

Henry said, "Hi, Annie. Who's your friend?"

"This is Baby Ruth Carson. They call her that because her grandmother is called Big Ruth, and her mother is called Little Ruth, so she's Baby Ruth. Baby Ruth, this is my brother—the one I told you about." Annie smiled sweetly at Henry. "The nice one."

Baby Ruth inspected Henry some more, through narrowed eyes, and Henry found himself

standing up a little straighter and pulling in his stomach.

"Did Baby Ruth just come in?" he asked, puzzled by the timing of her appearance—just before supper—which was an odd time to show up, unless you had been invited to supper. Baby Ruth snorted.

Annie said yes and gave him another big smile. "Baby Ruth is my guest . . . and Ma said we could. She's here for supper and to stay the night . . . dear Henry," she added, as an afterthought.

"I want to see you in the kitchen," Henry said. "Right now." He grabbed her by the upper arm and headed down the hall.

"You're hurting my arm," Annie squealed as the kitchen door shut behind them.

"When did Ma say you could have her over?"

"Last week."

"Well, she never told me."

"Well, she forgot."

"That was why you were so sickeningly sweet this morning, wasn't it?"

"I was not sickeningly sweet. I was just nice. Why can't you be nice?" she demanded.

Henry sagged in the middle. What was he getting so tensed about? So—the kid had a friend over. So what? One more hamburger and some giggling. She was entitled.

"All right. But if she's spending the night,

you're not going to stay awake talking and laughing till twelve o'clock and drive us all crazy and keep us all up, like you did the last time you had someone over. At eight-thirty it's lights out—right?"

"Nine."

"Eight-thirty. Or else."

Annie kicked the table leg. "All right. Eight-thirty. But Baby Ruth can stay up all night if she wants to, at her house."

"I don't care. I'll call you when dinner's ready."

Joe wandered in, looking for something to eat to keep him going while the hamburgers were cooking.

"Can't you just wait a minute? Dinner's almost ready. And set another place, will you?"

"How come?"

"Annie's got a guest. A kid named Baby Ruth, yet. For overnight."

Joe said, "Baby Ruth Carson? A skinny kid—dark hair—mean as a snake?"

"I don't know how mean she is. I just said hello to her. But she is skinny and she has dark hair. She didn't say much."

Joe groaned. "That's her. I'm leaving. That kid's a menace. When she stayed overnight at Rudy Phelps's house, she glued their old Persian cat to the rug while it was sleeping."

"Well, we don't have a cat."

"Listen, Henry, don't close your eyes while that kid's in the house. When that Baby Ruth Carson comes around," Joe said darkly, "things happen. I'm going to round up all the matches."

When Henry asked her, his mother dimly remembered having told Annie that she could have someone over, sometime soon.

"Well, the someone is called Baby Ruth Carson, and the sometime is tonight. And dinner's ready."

"I'll be down in a couple of minutes. Have any problems?"

"No," Henry lied. "No problems." Since he was going to eat the hamburger that was all black on the bottom, he didn't figure it was worth mentioning. And the hot-fat burns were hardly noticeable, unless you looked closely at the backs of his hands. But leftover hot dog slices, floating around in vegetable soup, would have been a lot easier.

At the table, Baby Ruth Carson didn't say much except "Pass the meat," "Pass the potatoes," and "Pass the beans." Her dark eyes flickered constantly around the table, like a snake's tongue, and her mouth and fork worked together like a machine . . . up and in, up and in. Henry had never seen anyone go through food like that. Where she was putting it all, he did not know.

After dinner, she and Annie went back into the living room, and Joe, who had put all the matches he could find in a coffee can, high up in the kitchen cabinet, went in there to watch TV and keep an eye on them.

Henry sat back, relaxed and satisfied. He'd gotten through two whole days now, with only a few minor setbacks—the burns on the kitchen linoleum, a little food thrown out, the hot-fat burns, and Throckmorton's appearance at school. Ma was getting all the free time and quiet she could use. And every day now, it would get better and easier because he was learning a lot.

His reverie was interrupted by a shout and a high, thin wail, coming from the direction of the living room.

Chapter Five

Friday   June 4

WHEN HENRY GOT TO THE LIVING ROOM, JOE was crouched at one end of the sofa—and Baby Ruth Carson was poised at the other. As he watched, they circled the sofa, each glaring at the other.

Annie, standing back by the fireplace, was wailing like a banshee.

Henry grabbed Joe. "You can't hit a little girl." He turned towards Annie, but kept a firm grip on Joe. "Annie, shut up. Please Annie."

Annie lowered her pitch just a little, but kept on screeching.

"Listen, Annie—if you don't shut up, I'll turn Joe loose." Henry figured she was worried about Baby Ruth, not afraid for Joe.

Annie subsided into deep sobs and hiccups. He'd guessed right.

From over their heads, Henry heard the attic door open. "Is everything OK down there?" his mother called.

Henry yelled, "Everything's just fine."

The door shut.

"Now," he said, turning back to Joe, "you want to tell me what happened here?"

"I was just sitting there on the sofa, and Annie got up and wanted to change the program to some dippy little cartoon show—and I said she couldn't."

"And?"

"And she did it anyway, and I said something to her and tried to change back to *Animal World*."

"And?"

"He called me a little pig," Annie said, snuffling. "He's not supposed to call me that."

41

"And?" Henry persisted, looking at Joe.

"And the next thing I know, that . . . that little devil over there had yanked my arm up behind my back and pulled my hand apart, practically. She had my hand up past my shoulder blades, Henry, and I thought she'd broken my fingers. It was like jungle warfare! She's probably ruined my throwing arm. For life."

"She's just a little girl," Henry said, very softly. "Take it easy. We don't want her telling her family that you tried to hurt her, Joe."

"Are you kidding? They'd probably cheer." He peered around Henry at Baby Ruth. "Touch me again, kid, and I'll let you have it."

Baby Ruth sneered. "You don't scare me. I have a little brother who could beat you up."

Joe pulled against Henry's grasp. "Just let me smack her one time, Henry."

"No way. You leave her alone." Henry turned back to Baby Ruth. "And you leave him alone."

"Don't worry. I won't touch him again," she said. Henry noticed that she put all her emphasis on *him*. It sounded as if she had something else in mind. He said, "OK, now I'm going to let go of you, Joe, but you've got to promise you won't touch her."

Joe said nothing.

"Look, we can't stand here all night. Come on. Say you'll leave her alone."

"OK. I'll leave her alone."

Henry released Joe and sat down on the sofa. Annie pulled out a bean bag chair for herself and one for Baby Ruth. Joe sat down beside Henry, and the crisis had passed. But every so often Henry, who was watching Baby Ruth pretty closely, caught her smiling to herself, and that made him distinctly uneasy.

When Henry went up to say good-night to his mother at eleven, Annie and Baby Ruth had been quiet for an hour, and Joe was safely asleep in his room . . . with his chest of drawers pushed up against the door.

Henry's mother looked tired and worried. He could see that she was sketching with a charcoal pencil. She closed the notebook as he came to the top stair.

"How's it coming, Ma?"

"I don't really know, Henry. I guess it's too early to tell."

"Can I see?"

She shook her head. "I know it sounds silly, but I don't want to show anyone what I'm doing at this stage. Maybe not until it's finished."

"That's OK. I can understand that."

"By the way, Aunt Wilhemina called today. She was very interested and supportive when I told her about Mr. Bennett and the job."

Henry grunted.

"So," his mother hurried on, "I asked her to drop by for supper Monday night. I told her you were going to be our chief cook and bottle washer for two weeks—and that you were doing a good job. Don't feel you have to fuss, dear—just set another place."

"She didn't believe the 'good job' bit?"

"Of course she believed it. Why shouldn't she? She just said how long it had been since we'd all spent some time together . . . and how you were all growing up so fast . . . and how lonely it was, sometimes, always eating by herself. I could hardly not invite her, dear."

"She says that all the time."

"Well, it's true, all the time. Look, if you don't feel up to it, I'll take Monday afternoon off, and . . ."

"No. You shouldn't do that. Then Aunt Wilhemina would think I couldn't handle it . . . and I can. We don't want her getting the wrong idea."

"All right. But you know you can always call on me."

"You just concentrate on drawing. I'll fix dinner on Monday—and it'll be terrific. No problem."

Henry went back down the attic stairs slowly, in deep thought. Aunt Wilhemina for dinner! This was going to be very tricky. He wouldn't want her to think that Joe and Annie—not to mention his mother—had to live on hot dogs and hamburgers. But, if he got too fancy and fell on his face, he'd wish he'd stuck with hot dogs and hamburgers. Yes, sir—it was going to be very tricky.

Baby Ruth and Annie were up early Saturday morning. Henry had expected them to spend the morning watching cartoons in the living room, but as soon as they'd had breakfast, Baby Ruth invited Annie to go back to her house with her. Thirty minutes later, they were gone. Henry was just sitting down, ready to relax at last, when Joe came into the living room and announced that he was leaving, too. "We're having softball practice. I'll be gone all morning."

"OK."

"Where's my glove?"

"How would I know? It was over there in the corner with your other stuff, yesterday."

Joe dug down through his comic books, sweat shirts, Frisbees, and fishing tackle. "Well, it isn't here now."

"So—look for it somewhere else."

Henry settled back once again. He'd watch a little television—maybe have a doughnut and some milk—and then he might call Charley Weideberg and see if he'd like to go to a movie after lunch. There was a science fiction double feature at the Cinema. The rest of the day was looking good.

He heard Joe come galloping down the stairs, but he didn't think much of it till Joe rounded the corner into the living room and held out, for Henry's inspection, a baseball glove that appeared to be leaking globs of melted cheese.

Chapter Six

Saturday   June 5

FOR A MINUTE, Joe struggled to get some words out, but Henry couldn't make any sense out of them. It wasn't so much that Joe was stuttering or babbling. It sounded more like he was being choked. Then, finally, Joe got his tongue sorted out, and the words could be heard and understood perfectly.

"I'm going to kill her. Look what she did to my glove. That little twerp! I can't wait to get my hands on her. She's going to pay."

"Who? What are you talking about? And what's that coming out of your glove? It's getting all over the rug."

"It's glue, that's what it is. She filled my glove

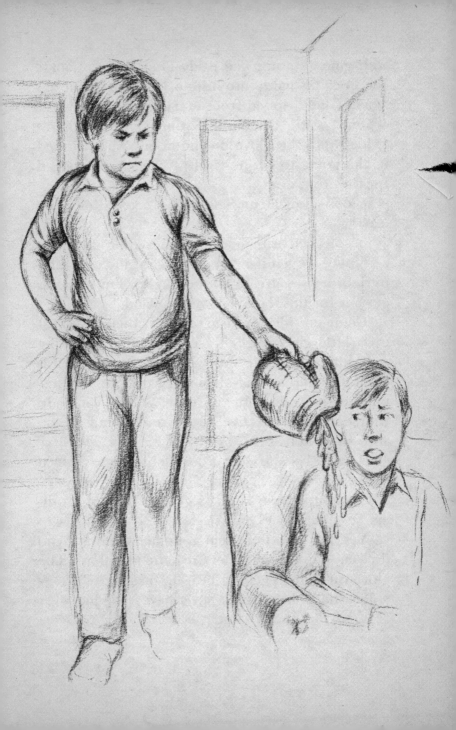

with glue . . . just like Rudy Phelps's cat. Look!" Joe stuck his hand into his glove and pulled it out again. Glue dripped from every finger.

Henry said, "It looks like your hand is rotting."

Joe flung the glove on the floor. "She's ruined it. I'm going to get her." He swiveled and started for the front door.

It took all of Henry's strength to keep Joe from leaving.

Joe pleaded with him. "It'll never be the same . . . never. Even if I can get all the glue out—and most of it's set already in the fingers. I'm going to get her for this, Henry. Swear to God."

"Come on, Joe. You can't go over there and beat up a little girl." He felt a certain fatigue coming over him. Either he was wearing out or Joe was getting better at this—from practice. In another minute, Joe might break loose. Henry came up with the most effective lie he could think of on such short notice.

"Annie says she's got a lot of brothers. They'd kill you."

Joe went limp in Henry's grasp. "A *lot* of brothers?"

"Yes. And most of them are older than us. Who do you think taught her to fight like that? The glove isn't worth getting beat up over, is it?"

Joe shook his head. "She's never coming over

here again, Henry. You've got to tell Annie. Never, ever, again."

"I'll talk to Annie," Henry promised. "I'm sorry, Joe. Maybe you should have collected all our bottles of glue, instead of our matches."

"That wouldn't have done any good," Joe said sadly.

Henry nodded. Joe was right. A kid like Baby Ruth Carson would probably keep a supply of glue always on her, like Jesse James always wore his gun.

He stayed up late Saturday night, watching TV The movie wasn't that good—but he hated to go to bed early on a night when he could stay up late. Finally, he was too tired to care. He climbed the attic stairs to say good-night.

His mother had fallen asleep. She was sitting at her desk, but her head was resting on her sketch pad. He hated to wake her, but if he didn't she might stay like that all night and catch cold, or get stiff or something.

"Ma—wake up."

"Oh? Gosh—I must have dozed off."

"You'd better go to bed in your bed."

"Right." She stood up slowly. "I'll never make it if I keep falling asleep like this."

He heard her door close as he climbed into bed.

He lay there in the dark, unable to sleep. For the first time, it occurred to him that she really might not make it . . . that she might fall asleep too many times and make too many mistakes and not have enough time . . . what then?

The weekend went by slowly. Having worked on his glove all day Saturday to no avail, Joe spent Sunday doing odd jobs to earn money to start a fund for a new one. Annie had called home late Saturday and asked if she could spend the night at Baby Ruth's. She got permission, although both Joe and Henry felt that letting Annie spend more time with Baby Ruth was just asking for trouble. So Annie was gone until late Sunday afternoon.

Henry spent a lot of his time thinking about that Monday night dinner with Aunt Wilhemina. He had to organize this perfectly—and make a big impression. If Aunt Wilhemina sensed for one moment that Henry couldn't handle things while his mother was busy, she'd be settled into that back bedroom before he could say "We're doing fine."

He decided on baked potatoes—which sounded real easy. You just put them in the oven and turned on the heat. And green peas, as a change from green beans. And soup—out of a can, of course. And something called Veal Chop Parmigiana, which looked terrific in a color picture in the cookbook. He wrote out the shopping list and gave it to his mother, who had to go into town Monday anyway.

Sunday night, he was forced to do some laundry because Monday was a school day, and the only clean clothes left in the house were pajamas and bathing suits.

Putting it in the machine wasn't so bad—and drying it was no big deal—but folding it and sorting it and getting everything to the right room was a real pain in the neck. If Henry could have had his way, he'd have dumped it all in a pile on the sofa and invited everyone to pick out his or her own things.

━━━◆━━━

Chapter Seven
Monday June 7

WHEN HE CAME HOME FROM SCHOOL MONDAY, the stuff for the dinner was all there—waiting for him in the kitchen. He checked on each ingredient, like a general making sure of his troops before a battle. Then he started Annie on the table setting right away—in case it had to be done and redone, over and over. He assigned the potatoes and soup to Joe, and he rolled up his sleeves to tackle the Veal Chop Parmigiana, himself.

Mixing the crumbs and grated cheese and seasonings in one bowl went well. Beating the egg in another bowl went fairly well, except for a little egg which slopped over onto the counter, so he had to add another egg, to make up. But when he tried dipping the first chop into the egg and then into the crumby mixture, he ended up with a chop, five fingers, and a bowl all coated with a thick layer of gritty yellow glop. It dropped off his fingers onto everything around him. When he tossed the coated chop into the skillet, it made a terrifying sizzling sound, and the yellow glop started to bubble and swell up around the chop as if it were alive. It sure didn't look like anything you'd want to eat. It looked, he thought, more like something that might eat you.

The next chop went into the egg satisfactorily, but when he dipped it into the wet, crumby mixture, it took most of what was left in the bowl—which meant that he'd end up with two covered-up chops and three naked ones—unless he did something. He tossed the second chop into the skillet, turned the first one over because it was already smoking a little, and made up a new batch of crumbs and seasonings. By this time, the second side of the first chop, and the first side of the second chop were smoking. He took the first one out of the skillet, turned the second one, and started dipping the third. He had the feeling that things were moving too fast for him, in a nightmarish sort of way, but he was determined not to yell for help. By the time he had the fourth and fifth chops browned, sweat was collecting in big drops on his brow and running down into his eyes. There was a whole crop of new hot-fat blisters on his hands, and the kitchen counter, sink, and floor were splattered with what looked like fast-setting, yellow cement.

He put all the chops back into the skillet with a sigh of relief. He covered each chop with a thick slab of cheese, poured tomato sauce over everything, and put a lid on it. Now the worst was over, and in forty-five minutes he would be serving dinner, triumphantly.

Aunt Wilhemina arrived early. He knew the minute she walked in, because he could hear her all the way at the back of the house. Heck, the people down at the corner could probably hear her. She came into the kitchen right away, and Henry was awfully glad that he'd spent some time scraping and wiping away the mess left over from the chops.

She sniffed the air like an old-fashioned movie detective. "Ah, ha! Macaroni and cheese. Am I right?"

"No, ma'am."

"No? Well then, burning rubber tires"—and she laughed a hearty laugh that made Henry's head ache.

"It'll be ready in a few minutes, Aunt Wilhemina. I'll have Annie call you and Ma when it's on."

"Where is your mother? Haven't seen hide nor hair of her. Joe let me in."

"She's upstairs—in the attic. No one's supposed to go up, though—she doesn't want us to bother her . . . she's awfully busy."

"Nonsense, Henry. I guess she'll always be glad to see her old Aunt Wilhemina."

"The thing is, she might be in the middle of something—she might not want to lose her thought."

"She just said that so you children wouldn't be constantly pestering her. I'm sure she's always made me feel welcome. I'm glad to say . . ."

The kitchen door slammed behind her, but Henry could still hear her as she started up the stairs.

". . . and I hope the day will never come when Ellen Walker makes her old Aunt Wilhemina feel unwanted and unloved."

Henry groaned. This was going to be a long supper.

Joe came into the kitchen. "I'm starved. Isn't it ready yet?"

"Yes, it's ready. Put one chop on each of those plates over there. I'll get the potatoes."

Henry had the potatoes in his oven mitt and was starting to deal them out onto the plates, when Joe caught his arm.

"Henry, I can't get them to let go."

"What are you talking about?"

"These chops. They won't come loose."

"Don't be silly. Use a spatula."

"Listen, Henry, I've *been* using a spatula. They're not even budging."

Henry put the last potato down and seized the spatula from Joe's hand. He tried to slip it under the nearest chop. It wouldn't go in, at any angle. The chop appeared to be solidly welded to the pan. Henry tried again . . . nothing. He could hear Aunt Wilhemina in the dining room. "Do you suppose the boys need help? Maybe one of us should go in and see how things are coming."

He strained to catch his mother's response. "Oh, I'm sure they've got everything under control. Tell me—what's Cousin Eloise doing these days?" She was trying to give them time and space to finish dinner by themselves. She really was the best mother he'd ever known. But she wouldn't be able to hold Aunt Wilhemina forever. It would be like trying to stop a Sherman tank.

He went into the pantry and got his father's hammer and screwdriver. He placed the tip of the screwdriver between the chop and the skillet and hit the end of the screwdriver with the hammer. Hard. The chop rocketed up into the air and sailed across the kitchen to the floor in front of the sink. Joe bent down and picked it up and burned his fingers. He dropped it into the sink.

"What'll we do?" he whispered.

Henry was busy positioning his screwdriver again. "Wash it off."

"Wash it?"

"Wash it. That's dinner."

Joe turned on the water. "It looks funny . . . sort of patchy, and gray in spots"

"Dry it off and put it on a plate. Heads up!"

Joe looked up and caught chop number two with his right eye. It took Henry a couple of minutes to get him cleaned up and calmed down. His eye appeared to be unharmed . . . just a little red and puffy.

"OK. Now, I'm going to go after the rest. And

this time, keep your eye on the chop instead of the chop on your eye."

"That's not funny, Henry."

"Well, anyway, catch them. I don't want them skidding around all over the floor. They'll get dirty."

"I could catch them a lot better if I still had my glove."

Henry stared into the bottom of the skillet when the last chop had been laid on its plate. "Where do you suppose the sauce's gone to?"

"I don't know. They look kind of funny, don't they?"

"Put the peas over them."

"You're kidding!"

"Put the peas over them and take them in before they get any colder. Just act natural."

"OK. But you do the explaining."

Aunt Wilhemina said, "I don't know that I've ever seen veal served quite like this . . . under a blanket of green peas. But it's very nice . . . just a little odd-looking. What do you call it?"

Henry was caught off guard. A name. He needed a name for this . . . this glop. He looked up and saw Joe's puffy, red eye, and the perfect name popped into his mind. "I call it Heads Up Veal," he said.

Joe choked.

As Aunt Wilhemina was putting on her coat to go, she said, "Before I leave, where is my darling Annie? I have a little something for her."

Joe was dispatched to pry Annie loose from the TV. When she came into the front hall, Aunt Wilhemina grabbed her and hugged her and handed over a chocolate bar that looked, to Henry, about the size of a compact car.

Annie's eyes bugged out and she said thank you at least fifty times, as she tore off the wrapper.

Aunt Wilhemina gazed at her and patted her on the head. "She must be such a comfort to you, Ellen."

Henry's mother said, "Well, yes, of course—we all love Annie."

Henry wondered if Aunt Wilhemina figured Annie made up for him and Joe . . . a sort of mother's consolation prize.

Next, Aunt Wilhemina clutched Joe and murmured, "The image of his dear father. The very image," and shoved a five-dollar bill into his hand. "Put this toward that new baseball glove, Joseph." She looked at him again, as if he were bleeding to death on the carpet, and said, "Poor lamb."

Joe said she didn't have to give him the money—about twice. Then he gave that line up and switched to thank you, before she could change her mind.

Finally, Aunt Wilhemina turned to Henry and

said, "I'm sure you'll find this very helpful, Henry." It was a small pocket dictionary. "I noticed that there were quite a few misspelled words in your last thank-you note and, of course, you'll never get to college that way."

Henry said thank you through tightly clenched teeth, because he had to. If he didn't *say* it, he'd have to write it—which would mean another thank-you note.

He stopped in at Joe's room on his way to bed.

"Thanks for helping out."

"You're welcome. It tasted OK. It really did."

"Yuh. How about that Aunt Wilhemina? She really gets me going."

Joe tucked his five-dollar bill into his piggy bank and put the bank back up on the shelf. "That's what I can never figure, Henry. I think it would be great having her here for a while. She could take over the cooking and all that stuff."

"She could take over us!"

"Well, I don't see it that way—and if it ends up with her coming, then that's all right with me. I don't like cooking and cleaning up and getting hit in the eye with a veal chop."

"I said I was sorry."

"And another thing. If Ma or Aunt Wilhemina had been around, Baby Ruth would never have filled my glove with glue."

"Listen, Ma's not God. She can't be everywhere. Baby Ruth might still have gotten to your glove."

"No, she wouldn't. Because she wouldn't have dared. Kids know. If Ma or Aunt Wilhemina had been around, my glove would not be out in the trash tonight."

Henry slammed the door on his way out. He felt as if he were floating through tropical seas on an iceberg that was melting fast. Eight days to go. Would the iceberg last?

———◆———

Chapter Eight

Monday   June 7

HIS MOTHER had been running her hands through her hair—a sure sign she was trying to solve a problem. Her hair stood out from her head as if she had been plugged into a socket.

Henry said, "I thought I'd say good-night."

"Good night, dear. The dinner went very well, really. You did a bang-up job."

"Thanks. Don't have her over again too soon, though. It's kind of a strain."

"Yes. I understand."

"How's the drawing coming?"

"Oh, I don't know. I had a couple of ideas, but every time I take another look at them, they lose something. I don't know if I'll ever settle down and get something done that I can hand to Mr. Bennett." She ran her hand through her hair again. "I've got lots of ideas. It's just that none of them are any good. And I haven't got enough time."

"Maybe if you took a break . . ."

"No breaks! That's the trouble with me, Henry. Every time things get rough, I take a break or fall asleep—and I lost a lot of time tonight—with Aunt Wilhemina here."

Henry thought he would just leave her alone. He didn't seem to be helping.

"Good night, Ma."

"Good night, dear."

Tuesday was one of those threatening days. Heavy clouds slid across the sky. Now and then, a gust of hot wind turned the leaves on the trees so their undersides showed. A faraway rumble of thunder sounded a warning. Henry hated days like this one—they always made him feel jumpy. He spent the afternoon in his room reading and eventually fell asleep.

He woke up, sweaty and headachey, and found a large, black cat sitting on his chest, glaring at him out of round, yellow eyes.

———◆———

Chapter Nine

Tuesday   June 8

HENRY HAD NEVER particularly liked cats. But he hadn't been really afraid of them till one clawed him badly while he was playing with it, and caused an infection that nearly cost him an arm. After that, whenever a cat came too close, Henry felt a sort of panic grab him.

Off to his left, a voice piped up. "See my new cat, Henry? This is Kitty."

"Get the cat off me, Annie," Henry said, being very careful not to move his lips—or any other part of his body. "Get him off me, Annie."

"Don't you like my cat, Henry?" Her head came into view on his left. She studied the cat as he sat, unblinking, on Henry's chest. "He likes you."

"Get him off me, Annie, or I will kill you."

"Boy, Henry, you're no fun. I thought you'd be

surprised, seeing Kitty sitting on your stomach like that—and you just lie there and say mean things to me. If you're not nice to us, Kitty and I won't like you anymore, will we, Kitty?"

Kitty flexed his claws, and Henry felt as if he were receiving about a dozen shots simultaneously. That did it. The paralysis which had held him motionless on the bed melted in the face of even greater fear and pain. With one violent bound, he knocked Kitty off his chest and scrambled to his feet. Less than a second later he was standing out in the hall, breathing hard. On the floor, Kitty gave out with a long, low gutteral squawl. He sounded to Henry like a cat who was cursing.

Annie demanded, "Why'd you hit him? You had no right to hit poor Kitty. I'm going to tell Ma."

"Oh, really? Well, while you're at it, tell Ma he sank his claws into my chest about an inch deep."

Annie went around the bed and scooped up Kitty, who draped himself over her arm like a thick, black shawl.

"Poor Kitty, did he hurt you?" she asked and marched out past Henry, who was inspecting his stomach and chest.

Suddenly, Henry realized she was headed for the attic. He tore down the hall and cut her off at the foot of the attic stairway, with her hand on the doorknob.

"Don't you dare go up there right now and bother Ma about this."

"You hurt my cat."

"That is not your cat. We are not keeping any cat. Especially that cat. No cats. We don't need a cat. We don't want a cat. No cats."

"Ma!" Annie yelled, "Ma, can I come up?"

Henry clapped his hand over her mouth. "Don't yell, Annie. Ma doesn't want to be disturbed."

Annie's front teeth came together hard on the inside of Henry's third finger. He turned her loose and yelled himself. Almost immediately, he could hear his mother start down the attic stairs.

For about two minutes, Annie gave her version of what had happened, and Henry, in the interest of truth and self-preservation, corrected her—point by point. Finally, his mother had had enough. "I don't *care* what happened," she said, "I've got to get back to work. Everyone seems to be overreacting to all this, anyhow. No more!"

There was a moment of silence while Annie caught her breath. Mrs. Walker took advantage of it to recommend alcohol for Henry's puncture wounds, and soap and water for his finger—and she sent Annie and Kitty to Annie's room to "rest" until supper was ready . . . whether they wanted to rest or not.

Henry doctored his injuries and then wandered

downstairs to the kitchen. He actually found it kind of soothing to get involved in cooking dinner. It took his mind off cats.

Annie opened her campaign at the dinner table. "There's going to be a terrible storm tonight. The man on the TV said so."

Immediately, Henry knew where she was headed. "Thunder showers. Maybe. That's all. And if you're leading up to keeping that cat, you can forget it."

Annie turned toward her mother. "I found him in the woods . . . between here and Baby Ruth's, and Baby Ruth says he was just moping around their place for a long time till their dogs nearly killed him."

Her mother said, "Poor thing. I wonder who he belongs to."

"He belongs to me now, because I fed him—and he loves me." She leaned forward, confidentially. "He hates Henry because Henry hit him, but he loves me."

Henry said, "I didn't hit him. I shoved him—a little—to get him off my chest."

"Wouldn't it have been nicer to simply pick him up and put him down on the floor?" his mother asked.

"No. She had no business parking him on my

chest while I was asleep. He might have . . . done anything. Who knows? You can't trust a cat."

"That's not true. Cats are very trustable. I trust him. And I'm going to keep him."

"*You* trust Baby Ruth Carson," Henry said. He turned to his mother. "I rest my case."

"Well, anyhow," Annie said, "I'm going to keep him."

"The hell you are. Not in this house."

Mrs. Walker raised her hand and her voice simultaneously. "That is enough! No more swearing, Henry. Annie—no more whining. And please—no more fighting. We're going to eat our dinner quietly and give this some thought. I'm very tired—and we're all hot. No more."

"I just want to know where that cat is right now," Henry said.

"Henry—didn't you hear me? I said we'd talk about it later."

Henry looked at Annie. She was watching the drapes at the side of the dining room window. Henry followed her gaze. He might have known it! Sitting behind the edge of the drapes, watching Henry, was a very large, black cat.

His mother was seated at her desk, with her chin in her hands. She didn't even turn towards him as he came up the stairs.

68

"Things not going well, Ma?"

Now she turned. "Yes. Things are not going well. As a matter of fact, things are terrible. TERRIBLE. My drawing is awful. My ideas are boring. This whole project is a waste of time."

"Sorry, Ma."

"How did I ever get myself into this?" she demanded.

Henry thought he would retire, before she gave that any more thought. "Good night, Ma."

"Good night."

When Henry got home on Wednesday, he came into the house cautiously. If that cat was still hanging around, he wanted to see it before it saw him. No cat. He breathed a sigh of relief. He was hungry and hot and tired—and in no mood to play games with a twenty pound "Kitty."

He had just finished his snack when the phone rang. He got it on the second ring . . . which was pretty good, from a sitting position. He hoped it hadn't disturbed his mother.

It was his Aunt Wilhemina.

"Hi, Aunt Wilhemina."

"Oh, yes—Henry." She said it as if he were a letdown and not what she'd been hoping for. "Is your mother there?"

"Well, not really. She's up in the attic working.

Can you call her back at suppertime, when she comes down anyway?"

"Well, I guess if that's the best we can hope for, we'll have to make do."

"Yes, ma'am."

"How is Annie? And Joseph?"

"They're fine. Joe's down the street hitting balls, and Annie's outdoors, probably playing with some dumb cat she found."

"How sweet! And is she going to be allowed to keep it?"

"I hope not."

"Really, Henry, you amaze me. Most children like animals. Why don't you like animals?"

Henry decided that if he couldn't bring himself to admit he was afraid of cats to his own mother and sister, he sure wasn't going to admit it to Aunt Wilhemina. He would bluff his way through. "I like animals, all right. It's just *this* cat. It's got a mean streak. You can tell by its eyes."

"Nonsense, Henry. Cats indicate their moods with their tails."

Henry wondered, privately, how come someone who knew so much about animals, and loved them so much, never got around to owning one of her own.

"Well, then, it's got a mean streak in its tail."

"Henry! Are you being fresh to me?"

"Heck no, Aunt Wilhemina. I just meant that the cat looked mean."

"I see." She sounded very stiff. Bad sign. "Very well. I shall call back tonight at six . . . to speak with your mother, if that meets with your approval."

"That'll be a good time. She's usually down by then."

"Good-bye." She hung up. Loudly.

Actually, his mother came down at quarter of six, and right away he told her about Aunt Wilhemina's call, so she'd be prepared. "She got a little huffy towards the end, Ma."

"Oh? Why?"

"I don't know. Something about my not trusting Annie's cat."

"Really, Henry, you're getting a little paranoid about that cat. You know that, don't you?"

"Lots of people don't like cats, and they're not all crazy."

His mother sat down wearily. "I just mean that you're overdoing it. Annie's very fond of the cat—and it's been perfectly well behaved with her. Can't you bend a little, and get to know it better? You might even get to like it."

Henry could feel the soles of his feet and the palms of his hands sweating now. "I don't want to get to know it better. I don't want it around me, Ma. Please."

His mother looked up at him for a minute. "OK. Let's compromise. If she keeps the cat outside during the day, until she goes to bed, how's that?"

"What happens when she goes to bed?"

"Well, maybe she could let the cat in then, and put it in her room till morning. It can't bother you in her room."

Henry stood there, silent.

"Be reasonable, Henry. That cat hasn't done anything so terribly wrong, so far—and Annie loves it." She grinned at him. "Throckmorton's gotten us all into a lot more trouble than that cat has, and he's just a frog."

"OK. I'll go along with what you said. But I don't want to have anything to do with that cat."

The phone rang. "That'll be her," Henry said.

"You are in a mood this evening, aren't you?" She went to get the phone.

Henry gave up on his science report at eight-thirty, even though it was due in two days. By nine, he was ready for bed. He was beat. He climbed the attic stairs slowly.

"I'm on my way to bed, Ma. You should go to bed, too. You're looking kind of tired."

"Do you realize I've used up one whole week, Henry? One whole week—out of two?"

"Well, that means you've still got a whole week left."

She nodded gravely. "Even if I work night and day, it won't be enough time."

"You're not going to bed now, are you?"

"No."

"Well, see you."

Chapter Ten

Thursday   June 10

IT STARTED OUT TO BE a morning just like any other. Henry got the lunches ready to go, found Annie's nickel for milk, and everyone was chomping away on their cereal. Then Annie stopped shoveling it in long enough to say, "I've got to be a green pea tonight, Henry."

Henry looked at her. "What do you mean, 'be a green pea'?"

"I mean," she explained patiently, "that for our class play tonight, I have to be a green pea."

"And?"

"And, I need a green pea costume."

Even Joe stopped eating. Henry said, "You're kidding! By tonight?"

"I told Ma. Way back. When I first got my part."

Joe said, "You dummy! You should have said something."

Annie said, "Well, I'm saying it now, aren't I?" Her voice trembled. "You can make me a costume, can't you, Henry?"

Henry said, "Sure thing, kid. Now hurry up or we'll miss the school bus." He simply had no idea of where to begin changing his sister into a green pea, so he decided to shelve the whole business till after school. Maybe, if he was lucky, lightning would hit the school—or him—by then.

By three o'clock, almost in spite of himself, he'd given it a lot of thought. Actually, it had sort of preyed on his mind. And he'd figured out one thing for sure. There was no way he could convert Annie into a single green pea. She'd end up looking like a giant green basketball . . . and how would they get her to school in that shape? She'd never fit into the car. They'd have to roll her down the hill into town. So—she had to go as a pea pod instead . . . and the place to start was with a pair of her sleepers. He'd dye her one-piece sleepers green. His mother had a whole drawerful of odds and ends of dyes. She'd have green in there somewhere.

She did. The box said "olive green," but Henry figured that was close enough. He mixed up the dye in the family spaghetti pot and threw in Annie's sleepers.

Half an hour later, he had an almost pea-green sleeper whirling madly in the dryer. Phase one was a success.

"So—you got her a green sleeper. Now what?" Joe asked.

"Well, I figure we'll sew the legs together—to make it look more like a pea pod—and maybe we'll sew the arms into the sides—and then we'll take a black felt-tip pen, and draw an opening, as if the pod had split open, and then we'll draw the peas inside.

Joe nodded. "Sounds good. Have fun."

"You sew."

"Come on, Henry. I never sewed anything in my whole life."

"Here's a big, fat needle and some nylon fishing line. Just start with a big knot and end with a big knot and take big stitches in between. It'll never show."

"And what will you be doing, while I do all the hard work?"

"I'll be cooking supper. We've got to get the kid there before seven."

There was no doubt about it. With her legs sewn

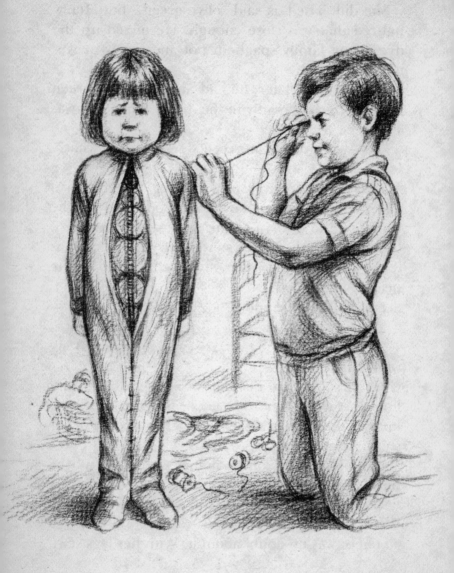

together, her arms down by her side, a split in her pod, and with the outline of the peas inside drawn in black, Annie made a great green pea pod.

Henry stood back. "Not bad. Not bad, at all."

"I think it's terrific. And next time, Annie, you'd better let us know sooner." Joe inspected his Band-Aided hands. "What do you bet I'm not able to throw in Saturday's game? And what'll I tell the guys?"

"Tell them you were pruning the roses. No one will ever know the difference."

Annie was not happy. "I can't move . . . just teeny, tiny steps."

"Well, all you have to do is stand there and say something, not do a song and dance number," Henry said.

"How'll I get up the school steps?" she whined.

Henry said, "We'll carry you. Take it off and sit down and eat your supper. I'll call Ma down."

Even Henry's mother was impressed. "Honestly, Henry, I couldn't have done better myself if I'd had a week to work on it."

Joe said, "Hey! Wait a minute. I did all the sewing."

She said, "You both did a beautiful job."

Joe said, "If they give you a choice next year, Annie, ask to be the green pea. Tell them you already got the outfit."

77

For speed's sake, Henry got on one side of Annie and Joe got on the other and they airlifted her out of the house and into the car.

They pulled into the parking lot at seven, sharp.

"We'll carry her up the stairs and deliver her backstage, Ma. You go and get some good seats in the auditorium."

"You look delicious, dear," she said and planted a kiss on the top of Annie's head.

"Are you ready?" Henry asked.

"Ready on this side," Joe said, and up she went.

Mrs. Corcoran was delighted with Annie's outfit. "You boys did all this yourselves?"

"Yes, ma'am."

"I wish you could outfit my whole cast."

Joe muttered something about not ever intending to sew anything, ever again, for anyone—but fortunately, Mrs. Corcoran didn't hear him.

Joe and Henry watched critically as the various fruits and vegetables assembled themselves on the stage. Mrs. Corcoran pronounced herself satisfied with the overall effect, and the fruits and vegetables were told to leave the stage to make way for the meat and dairy actors. Annie started to shuffle off.

"We'd better pick her up," Henry said, "or she'll still be on the stage when the bread group is finished."

They had the carrying bit down to a science. Annie was whisked off the stage in ten seconds flat. They stood in the wings and watched the other food groups go on and off stage, and commented on the various costumes with professional frankness. All three of them agreed that there wasn't as good an outfit in the whole cast as Annie Walker's pea pod.

Suddenly, it was seven-thirty. The house lights dimmed. The master of ceremonies came on and whipped through his introduction. It was time to go on. Annie started shuffling back onstage. All the other fruits and vegetables were in place, waiting . . . waiting . . . waiting for Annie. The master of ceremonies had quit talking. There was a rising buzz of anticipation or impatience coming from the audience. Henry could feel Annie's growing embarrassment. Her cheeks were turning bright red. She needed help quick.

"Pick her up," he whispered to Joe and moved towards her.

"Huh?"

"Pick her *up*!" he ordered, in his most carrying tone. The moment the words left his lips, he knew he'd made a mistake. Joe jumped forward, but so did the curtain raiser who went into action when he heard "*up!*"

The curtain started up as Joe and Henry staggered across the stage carrying Annie. A ripple of laughter flowed across the audience. Joe looked up and saw an auditorium full of people, all looking at him. He gasped and dropped his share of Annie.

"For God's sake, Joe, quit fooling around," Henry said, "I can't carry her by myself."

Joe gargled something incoherent and fled.

Henry leaned forward and said, "Stiffen up, kid." Then he grabbed Annie from behind by her shoulders, tilted her backwards, and slid her into her proper position on her slippery, sleeper soles as if she were a piece of furniture mounted on a dolly. When he'd stood her up straight once more, he patted her briskly on the back for encouragement and walked off.

Later, Mrs. Corcoran told him he'd gotten the biggest hand of the evening. Henry really hadn't noticed. He'd been searching for Joe. He had no clear idea of what he'd do to Joe when he found him, but he knew instinctively that it would be something painful.

Joe was nowhere to be seen for the rest of the performance, but as his mother left the auditorium, he appeared out of the crowd around her and took her arm.

"Can't be too careful in these crowds, Ma," he said.

Henry, on his mother's side, said, "I owe you one, Joe."

Joe didn't answer. He just tightened his grip on his mother's arm.

When they'd all tucked Annie in and were downstairs again, Henry asked, "Did I ever do that to you, Ma—need a costume the same day, or whatever?"

"You sure did. I remember once you had to be a tree. Oh, you'd gotten a notice to give to me, but you'd forgotten all about it, and then when you remembered, it was so close to the time, you were afraid to tell me. The teacher called me when you refused to go to the last rehearsal."

"What did you do?"

His mother laughed. "We dyed *your* sleepers brown—and strapped branches to your arms and your back."

"I don't really remember all this. Did you yell at me?"

"No."

"Why not? What a dumb thing to do. At least Annie told us herself this morning."

"Why would we yell? You felt bad enough already. Did you yell at Annie?"

"No. She just forgot. . . . I forget a lot of things. . . ."

She hugged him.

He hung around for a minute, trying to say it right.

"Ma—I don't want us to change."

She didn't answer right away. Then she said, "Everything changes, Henry."

———————◆———————

Chapter Eleven

Thursday   June 10

WHEN HENRY CAME UP the attic stairs around ten-thirty, his mother's back was towards him. She was studying a half-dozen sketches tacked to the wall. From that distance, Henry couldn't make out what they were. As he waited, she went around collecting the original six and tacked up six more. Again, she stepped back to study them.

Henry coughed.

She jumped.

"Goodness, Henry, how long have you been standing there?"

"Just a minute."

She whipped the sketches down from the wall and threw them onto her desk.

"Are you working on all of those?"

"No. Just trying to decide which ones to concentrate on."

"Then you're making a lot of progress, right?"

"Well, I've made a lot of beginnings, if that's what you mean. The question is, which, if any, will end up being worth something."

"You want me to take a look? Maybe I could help you decide."

"No. I'd really rather not have anyone else see them. Thank you."

"OK."

"You're not angry, are you, Henry?"

Henry said, "No. I'm not angry." But inside he felt hurt that she didn't want or need his advice. His advice wasn't welcome—but his cooking, cleaning, and thinking up crazy costumes at the last minute, *and* making lunches—that was OK. Sure—he could handle all the unimportant stuff— but just don't let him have an opinion on anything that meant something.

He started downstairs.

"Good night, Henry."

He closed the attic door on the tail end of her "Good night." Maybe she'd assume he just hadn't heard her.

Chapter Twelve

Friday   June 11

THE BEST THING YOU COULD SAY about this Friday, Henry thought as he climbed back up on the school bus, was that it *was* a Friday . . . and now, for two days, he didn't have to go to school.

It had been hot and sticky all day—and the history teacher had finally gotten around to giving them the big test they'd all studied for about ten days ago—only by now, most of the dates had sort of run together in Henry's mind . . . like melting chocolate candies. And he was tired. Tired of bologna for lunch, and hot dogs and hamburgers for supper, and cleaning up after. He was even tired of his own family. He deliberately picked a seat as far away as possible from Joe and Annie.

A large, black car was pulling into the driveway as they got off the bus. Henry groaned out loud. Just what he needed to make this day complete— Aunt Wilhemina. He thought he'd left the kitchen in pretty good shape that morning. The living room was full of newspapers and books, but he'd gone around Thursday afternoon and collected all the apple cores, sandwich crusts, and dirty glasses. All in all, the house wouldn't look too bad.

"Ah, Henry. And Joseph. And my darling Annie." She stood there, waiting for the standard hug and kiss. Annie trotted right over and went into her "dear Aunt Wilhemina" act . . . and Joe managed to peck her on the cheek and nudge her a little, but Henry couldn't do it. He just stood there, feeling hot and stupid and stubborn. If someone had offered him a hundred thousand dollars to go over there and kiss her and hug her, he couldn't have done it.

They all went in, and Aunt Wilhemina yodeled up to Henry's mother. The windows rattled in their frames. Naturally, his mother came down immediately. Her hair was standing out in wisps, and her face was very pink. She'd been asleep. Well, Henry thought, if you're going to work all night, you've got to get your sleep sometime. But he knew she didn't want Aunt Wilhemina to know. She kept trying to pat her hair back into place.

"I brought a few little things for the children," Aunt Wilhemina said. "When I heard about Annie's new kitten, I just had to bring over a little 'welcome' gift." She hauled out a paper bag and handed it to Annie.

Annie took out a catnip mouse, a sparkling, glittering rhinestone cat collar, and a white china cat figurine. Henry could tell she was really thrilled. She bounced around the room showing the collar to everyone, and then she ended up back at Aunt

Wilhemina and kissed her twice. Henry grunted.

"And now, for Joseph." And she handed Joe a large box. Joe tore the wrapping paper off and held it up. It was an oil paint set. "I've always thought Joseph showed real talent. Haven't you?" she asked Henry's mother.

"I don't know. It's possible. I know he'll love to work with the set. It was so nice of you."

Joe had the box open now, and was taking each item out and showing it off. Boring.

"And now, for Henry. Of course, he's older and not really a child anymore—a fact he never lets us forget. . . ." and she handed him a square, heavy box. He opened it with rising anticipation, in spite of himself. Maybe, this time . . .

It was soap. A big cake of soap, on a rope. to be used in the shower. And there was a bottle of men's cologne. The soap, and the paper lining of the box, were faintly yellowed. She'd gotten it at someone's yard sale or a flea market. For a dollar, maybe.

"Thank you."

"You're welcome."

Henry's mother caught his eye and, somehow in that instant, she managed to convey sympathy. So—she knew how he felt. His anger subsided a little. He picked up his soap and cologne and stood up. "I have to go upstairs. Thanks again, Aunt Wilhemina."

But she was already busy talking with Joe about what he would paint first. She didn't even hear him.

Upstairs, he opened the cologne. It smelled kind of sweet and heavy and sickening. He poured it down the toilet, and, diluted like that, it made the bathroom smell real nice for a while. The soap he threw into his bottom drawer. He wasn't going to wear a bar of soap around his neck like a dog tag. And he wasn't going downstairs again, till he saw her car pull out of the driveway.

Joe got down to the business of painting after dinner that same night. He arranged all his paints on the kitchen table. "She thinks I might grow up to be a painter."

Henry nodded.

"Why don't you try to do something, Henry? Don't you have any paints?"

"No."

"Maybe Henry could carve things," Annie said. "He's got a jack knife."

"Hey, that's a good idea. Come on, Henry—you carve and I'll paint."

"I don't have anything to carve, even if I wanted to."

"I'm going in to watch *Lucky Ladies,*" Annie said.

"Go, already." Henry sat down to watch Joe. It *would* be kind of fun to do something like that. He thought his old jack knife was in his bureau. Maybe he could whittle on something. He headed upstairs to get his knife.

He found it in the bottom drawer . . . and his eye fell on the bar of soap. That was what he'd whittle! Perfect! Aunt Wilhemina's bar of soap. He headed downstairs, humming one of Annie's sick little songs.

He wanted to do something that would symbolize Aunt Wilhemina. Something just like her. He looked around the kitchen, searching for an inspiration, and found it when he got to the cupboard. There was a box of Napoleon cookies. Napoleon! He would whittle out Aunt Wilhemina, as Napoleon.

He'd never had much luck carving before, but tonight the soap just seemed to fall away in the right places. By eleven, he was satisfied. He stopped and put his Napoleon down. Joe looked up.

"How'd it go?"

"Just fine."

"Can I see it now?"

Henry handed it over.

"This is Napoleon, right? With that hat. But it's a lady."

"Right."

"A nutty, fat lady—with her glasses on crooked and her hair in a bun in back."

"Right."

Joe looked at Henry. "That's not . . . This isn't Aunt Wilhemina?" He shook his head.

"Right."

Joe shook his head again slowly. "You shouldn't have done that, Henry. Out of her own soap." He was still shaking his head, but he was looking at the carving and grinning.

Henry started to clear away the soap chips. "Hand it over."

"If she ever knew . . ."

"She won't. Unless you tell her."

"I won't."

"You coming up?"

"I guess so." Joe put the lid on his set. "How come you hate her so much, Henry?"

"I don't hate her. I just don't like the way she comes at people, like a bulldozer, and I don't think she likes me. And if she moved in here, I'd be out."

"You're crazy. She couldn't push you out. Ma would never . . ."

Henry said, "She could make me want to go."

The attic stairs felt as if they were each about two feet tall.

"Hey, Ma!"

She looked up from her easel. "Henry. Is it that late?"

"Eleven-thirty."

"Gosh! I thought it was about nine."

"Are you going to quit for the night?"

"No. I can't stop now. It's coming along— I don't want to stop while things are going well."

"What if they go well till morning?"

"Then I'll just be grateful—and keep going with them."

Henry waved good-night and started down the stairs. He didn't know how she did it . . . even sleeping some during the day. Of course, she was looking awfully tired . . . which worried him. If something happened to her, what would they do? Well, only four more days and then Wednesday— and win or lose, it would all be over.

<hr/>

Chapter Thirteen

Saturday June 12

HE WAS DREAMING, and then he was waking up— or maybe he was still dreaming. Something was pursuing him—stealthily—watching, biding its time. He wasn't able to get away, and he was hardly able to bear being so frightened.

He forced himself to wake up, hoping for relief. The room was very dark. He heard, or thought he heard, small, cautious sounds from the floor near the foot of his bed. He strained through the darkness to see or hear what it was.

Silence. Whatever it was wasn't moving anymore. It was probably just waiting out there for him to move.

He couldn't stand it any longer. He reached over and snapped on his bed-table lamp. There was an instant response from the floor—Kitty leaped up on the foot of his bed and started walking across the quilt towards him.

He dared not move, but he could still talk. He said huskily, "No." And then louder, "No!"

The cat stopped and sat down. His big, golden eyes gleamed in the light from Henry's table lamp. He started to wash his lustrous black fur.

"Go away!"

The cat blinked and stretched and settled back down for more washing.

Henry said, "Please—go away."

Nothing. He just sat there staring at Henry, waiting.

Henry listened to the silence around him. Sometimes Annie or Ma or Joe got up to go to the bathroom or get some milk . . . but the house was as silent as any old house could be.

He was terrified, but he could not bring himself to yell for help and deliberately wake someone up. That would be too humiliating. If someone were already up, it was no big thing to call them into his room for a few moments of friendly conversation and cat removal—but screaming for help was OUT. Besides—what would he yell? "Help! There's a cat washing in here!" People would think he was crazy.

The cat got up and moved closer.

"No!"

He sat down and kneaded Henry's quilt with his claws, studying him solemnly. Henry watched the cat as if he were a smoking bomb.

Suddenly, Henry couldn't stand it. He had to get out of that room. He rolled out from under the covers and ran for the door. Now, he had the knob in his hand, and now, the door was shut. It was shut! And the cat was shut up inside his bedroom.

He walked away at a fairly normal pace. Down the stairs—careful going around Annie's newest pile of junk—and into the living room.

He curled up on the sofa. It wasn't very comfortable, but it was cat-free.

Henry woke up early Saturday morning. He felt as if he'd been sleeping on a sack full of tire irons.

Annie came down as he was trying to rub the kink out of his neck. "Annie—your cat is in my room."

"He is? I wondered where Kitty went."

"Get him out. And Annie—no more cats in the house at night."

"Ma said . . ."

"I don't care what Ma said. I say no more cats. That cat came into my room last night—and practically pushed me out of my own bed."

"Was that why you slept on the sofa, Henry?"

"The point is—you were supposed to keep that cat in your room so it wouldn't bother anyone else. You didn't. So he stays out at night from now on."

"You're mean. You're not like Ma or Aunt Wilhemina. And I wish you weren't in charge. I wish Ma or Aunt Wilhemina was in charge. They like cats."

"Listen, Annie—try to understand."

Annie walked out on him. "I miss my mother. And I'm going to tell her on you—that you're mean to me. And I'm going to tell everyone."

"Good! You do that. And while you're at it, take your damn cat out of my bedroom."

Henry sat back down on the sofa, with his head in his hands. He was feeling distinctly lonely. And tired. Here it was, just ten days since Ma had first seen that ad—and it seemed like ten years. And he still had four days to go.

By nine, Saturday morning, Annie was having withdrawal symptoms because she had no one her own age to play with. "Can't I have someone over?"

"I guess so. Who'd you have in mind?"

"Baby Ruth Carson."

"Oh, no! Have a heart, Annie. You know what happened last time."

"But Joe won't be home this morning. He's at softball practice. And we could lock up his room."

"No!"

"There's no one else," she wailed. "Everyone's going to do something with their mother. Mine's stuck up in the old attic."

Oh, boy, Henry thought, here it comes—the old "poor me" bit.

"Marlene is going shopping with her mother . . . and Beth Ann is making cookies with her mother . . . and Lorelei . . ."

"OK, already. I get the point. Listen, I have an idea. Why don't you go over to Baby Ruth's?"

"I can't. Her mother has a headache."

Henry nodded. "If I were Baby Ruth Carson's mother, I'd have a headache every day."

"Well, can I? Ask her over?"

Henry sighed. What with the War of the Cat flaring up again, he and Annie weren't on such great terms. Maybe, just this once, he should give in. "OK—but you keep an eye on her and so will I."

"Thank you, dear Henry. You are my very best brother and I love you."

"Stow it, Annie."

"I'll go call her right now."

When Baby Ruth Carson rang the bell at eleven, Henry made darn sure that he answered the door. She was wearing a pair of blue jeans and a red sweat shirt. Carrying no packages, that he could see.

"Hi, Baby Ruth."

She bobbed her head up and down in greeting or acknowledgment.

"I don't want to be mean or anything, but after last week—Joe's glove—I'll have to ask you to check your weapons at the door." He smiled and chuckled heartily, hating himself as he did it. How phony could you get! "If you're carrying anything on you—like glue, for instance—or just anything— you can leave it with me till you go."

Wordlessly, she reached up inside the folds of her sweat shirt, drew out a small, brown bag, and shoved it at him.

"Is this the lot?"

She nodded.

"OK. Thanks. And when you're ready to go, I'll be glad to give it back. OK?"

She didn't answer.

"No hard feelings?" he persisted. Somehow, in spite of Joe's glove, he felt awfully mean, acting like this to a little girl.

She looked up at him. "It's OK. Can I come in, now?"

"Sure. Come on right in," and he practically bowed. Well, at least he'd prevented another catastrophe.

He served them toasted cheese sandwiches and ice cream for lunch. Baby Ruth only ate one sandwich and barely tasted her ice cream. Henry made a mental note to ask his mother to buy a different brand of ice cream and to take the toasted cheese sandwiches off the heat a little sooner, next time.

At two-thirty, Annie came up to his room. "Baby Ruth's ready to go home now."

"OK. I'll get her bag."

He followed Annie downstairs and retrieved the little brown bag from the back of the highest shelf in the coat closet, where he'd hidden it. Annie came running down the hall.

"She's gone already!"

"She left? Without her bag?"

"Yes. I looked everywhere."

Henry stood there, holding Baby Ruth's bag. He felt like two cents. "Call her up as soon as she's had time to get home, and tell her she forgot her stuff. Maybe she didn't understand that I was going to give it back."

Annie nodded. She looked at Henry. "Poor Baby Ruth."

" 'Poor Baby Ruth'? How about poor Joe, huh? I was just trying to keep her from doing something else crazy."

Annie went to the phone. A few minutes later, she was back.

"It's for you."

"The phone?"

"No. The bag. She says it's something she made for you. And she's sick. That's why she went home early. I'll bet it was those sandwiches."

"Those sandwiches were all right. I ate two of them."

"How do you feel?"

"I feel fine. Just great." Even as he spoke, Henry experienced a small wave of nausea, but he made up his mind to ignore it.

"Open the bag, and let's see what she made you."

Henry knew it was silly, but just for a second or two, he didn't really want to open that bag. He knew it couldn't be anything dangerous, but still— he didn't want to open that bag. A small, poisonous snake would fit into a bag like that—or a tarantula—or even a small, very small bomb. He shook himself. Now he was just plain being crazy. He was talking about a little kid, for Pete's sake. He opened the bag.

━━━━━━◆◆◆━━━━━━

Chapter Fourteen

Saturday   June 12

IT WAS A COOKIE . . . wrapped up in layers and layers of tissue paper . . . a big, yellow cookie, with *Henry* spelled out in pink frosting letters. That was all. One very large, homemade cookie.

Henry said, "What do you know?"

Annie said, "She made it herself."

"Why? I, mean, I was never that nice to her. There's nothing wrong with it, is there?"

"No, there isn't, you mean person. You made Joe stop trying to get her—and you let me ask her over again. She doesn't get to come back lots of places. And I told her you were nice . . . and she likes you."

"Well, thanks—I guess."

"What'll you do with it?"

Henry looked at the cookie. It did not look appetizing. There were one or two smudges on it that were probably dirty fingerprints . . . and it was kind of thick and doughy in the center. He knew he could never eat it and enjoy it. But he could never just throw it out, either. He'd have to keep it, somewhere—at least for a while. On his mantel in his bedroom. "I'll put it on my mantel—as a souvenir. It's too big and pretty to eat."

Annie nodded, satisfied. "I'll tell her."

"Yuh. And tell her thanks—I really like it—and we hope she feels better."

"And maybe she can come over next Saturday, too?"

Henry knew when he was licked. "Sure thing."

He had to cough twice to get his mother's attention.

She waved her free hand, but didn't look up. "How's it going, Henry?"

"I thought I'd turn in now, Ma."

"OK. Good night."

"Ma, you should get more sleep."

"Henry, please don't fuss at me now. I'm right in the middle of something. I'll catch up on my sleep later."

He went downstairs without another word, feeling angry, hurt, and rejected, in spite of himself.

He put the cookie on his mantel Sunday morning. From a distance, it looked almost like a small plate with his name on it. But it looked kind of lonely up there, all by itself, so he dug out Aunt Wilhemina as Napoleon and put her up there, too. She balanced the cookie very nicely.

His mother noticed the carving when she came in to talk to him Sunday morning. She just said, "That's a very nice bit of whittling, Henry."

"Thanks, Ma."

Annie noticed it too, when she came in to have him read the funny papers to her.

"Did you do that, Henry?"

"Yes."

"Who is it?"

"It's Napoleon."

"It's funny. I like it."

"Thank you, Annie."

Henry was preparing to scramble some eggs for a sort of Sunday brunch when Annie came running into the kitchen.

"Henry! Henry! Baby Ruth's in the hospital!"

"You're kidding!"

"I'm not. She got awful sick, and then they had to take her to the hospital." She paused. "I told you those cheese sandwiches weren't good."

For a fraction of a second, Henry's heart

lurched to a full stop, and he wondered if somehow his cheese sandwiches had landed an innocent victim in the hospital. Then he got hold of himself and said, "They were just lightly browned."

"Well, Baby Ruth is in the hospital."

"I ate them. You ate them. We're OK, aren't we?"

Annie sat down, obviously unconvinced.

Joe said, "I've changed my mind. I don't want any eggs after all. I think I'll have some cereal."

"Fine. Have cereal—three times a day, for all I care. It'll be a lot easier for me."

Joe whispered something to Annie. She giggled.

"What did he say?" Henry demanded.

"He said it would be a lot safer for us."

Henry composed himself. "Counting today, only three more days, Lord. Just three more days." He didn't know if he could go another three days without hitting someone over the head with a skillet. It was almost a relief when Aunt Wilhemina called, late in the morning, to invite them all out for lunch. Almost.

Henry's mother accepted and insisted that Henry go, too, because she said it would be just too obvious if he didn't.

"Well, at least I'll get a good meal I didn't have to cook," he said.

"Is it getting too much for you, Henry?"

"No. Not at all. Ever. Everything's OK. You

know how I am—always complaining about something."

After a big meal at a restaurant, there was no way out. . . . Aunt Wilhemina had to be invited in. They all sat around in the living room and yawned and tried to keep talking. But they were too hot and too full and too sleepy.

Annie got up suddenly and disappeared. A few minutes later, she came back. She was carrying Napoleon, and she was headed directly for Aunt Wilhemina.

<hr />

Chapter Fifteen
Sunday   June 13

IT WAS JUST ONE OF THOSE THINGS Henry didn't have to think about. He got up and launched himself into a flying tackle at Annie in one swift motion. He missed. Annie looked down at him, as he lay there gasping for breath on the rug, and said, "My goodness, Henry—did you trip?" . . . and trotted on.

From his observation point—about an inch

above the nap of the carpet, he saw Joe make a wide, sweeping motion with his arm, as if to scoop Annie in, but although she was not built for speed, she was light on her feet. She danced nimbly out of his reach and said, "Cut it out, Joey—I want to show Aunt Wilhemina what Henry made."

His last hope was his mother. She said coaxingly, "What's that you've got there, dear? Why don't you show it to me, first?" but Annie ignored her and handed Napoleon to Aunt Wilhemina. "See what Henry did? He has too got talent."

There was a short silence. Henry, with his face buried in the rug, hoped it would go on forever . . . or until he suffocated, whichever came first.

"For heaven's sake, it's Napoleon! Quite recognizable, with that hat and all . . . Really very clever, Henry. Sort of a caricature, isn't it?"

Henry said, "Thank you. Yes, ma'am."

"Looks like real ivory, but it couldn't be. . . . What is it made of?"

Henry felt panicky and light-headed. He said, "Someone gave it to me. I don't know what all goes into it. It's very easy to carve."

Aunt Wilhemina leaned down and handed it back to him. "That's really very good, for a first effort. I can see that I underestimated you, Henry."

On his way back upstairs, Henry remembered that Napoleon had been a great strategist. He dropped the little carving in the bathroom trash basket with a shiver.

His mother was painting. She had pulled the green-shaded light down low over her easel. It lit. her hair up like a Christmas halo. The attic was dark all around her. He stopped on the top step, as usual.

"Hey, Ma. How's it going?"

"I don't know, Henry. I don't see how I can possibly get all this finished by Wednesday morning."

"Ask for more time."

"No. I won't ask for more time. He gave me till Wednesday, and I agreed, and it would be unprofessional to go back now begging for an extension. If I can't meet deadlines, I shouldn't be asking for this job."

"Well, I guess I'll go on to bed, now."

"Oh, Henry—one more thing. Aunt Wilhemina has offered to take you all shopping tomorrow after school. Everybody needs some summer things. She said she'd take you down before the stocks are all picked over. I'll give her my charge plates."

"I'll wait till you can go."

"But that might be weeks. You must be uncomfortable now, in this heat, wearing your regular school clothes."

"I'll wait."

"Henry, bend a little."

"She isn't going to want to buy me the kind of things I like to wear. She's out of touch, Ma, and she doesn't want to listen to me. And then I'd have all that stuff, and you'd have to pay for it, and I'd *have* to wear it."

His mother shook her head. "All right. Have it your way."

"Good night, Ma."

"Good night, dear."

Annie came into the kitchen Monday morning and adopted her "earthshaking news" pose—eyes opened wide and hands on hips. "Baby Ruth's had an operation. I just called her house and they told me."

"What'd they do?" Joe asked. "Did they take out her crazy bones or amputate her mean streak?"

"No. They took out her . . ." Annie rolled the word out very carefully, "ap-pen-dix."

"Then it wasn't my sandwiches after all, was it?" Henry said.

Joe said, "I don't know, Henry. I've heard that you can get a bad appendix from burned cheese sandwiches."

"Well I've heard that you can get a lump on your head from having a smart mouth," Henry said and he put the skillet down very carefully. "Do you want to make one last crack about my cooking and find out?"

Joe focused his attention on his plate. "Not me. I never did think you were such a bad cook."

"I'm going to make her a card—and send her a gift," Annie said.

Henry nodded. "That's real nice, Annie."

"But they won't let me in to see her. Mrs. Carson says I'm too little."

"Right."

"You have to be twelve."

"That's right."

"Why twelve?" Annie asked.

"Because," Joe said, "when you're little, you're full of germs and they want to keep you away from the sick people in case you make them worse."

"That's not right, is it?" Annie asked. "I'm not germy, am I, Henry?"

"The thing is, Annie—they think you might give her something that's going around at school. It's not your fault. It's like that everywhere."

"You're twelve," she said.

"Yuh. I'm twelve."

"So—you could take my gift and my card to Baby Ruth."

"No, I couldn't and I'll tell you why. Because I'm not taking anything to some little kid in the first grade."

Annie's lower lip began to tremble. "There isn't

anyone else, Henry. If you don't do it, she won't know I miss her."

"Come on, Annie, have a heart."

"She's all by herself, and none of her friends can visit her." Her voice wavered a little.

"Don't cry, Annie. We'll think of something."

A fat tear rolled past Annie's nose and down to her chin, where it clung precariously.

"Oh, brother," Joe said.

"I'll go, Annie. I'll go tomorrow afternoon. You've got to give her time to come out of the anesthesia and get to feeling a little better. You get the stuff together and I'll take it after school. But just once. Just one time."

"Thank you, Henry. You are my best brother." She cast a dark look at Joe. "I love you, Henry."

Henry said, "Stow it, Annie."

"Boy! The kids at school are going to get a kick out of this—my brother and Baby Ruth Carson."

"No they won't, because they won't know." Henry leaned down close to Joe. "Because, Joseph, if anyone ever breathes a word about this, I will tell Ma about that picture of that girl you cut out of that magazine in the barbershop . . . the one without any . . ."

Joe said, "Hey! I wouldn't tell. You know that, Henry. I'd never tell."

"Good."

"And you'd never tell either, would you?"

Henry said smoothly, "That all depends on you."

"How'd you find out about that picture, anyway?"

"Putting your laundry away, that's how. And if I found it, Ma will find it."

Joe got up. "I think I'll just go upstairs now," and he left. Henry heard him going up the stairs double-time. Annie bustled off, preparing for school. Henry was left alone to straighten up. So—now he was hooked to go and visit a little monster in the hospital. When he grew up, he was going to be a bachelor—forever.

He had supper ready and holding, before Aunt Wilhemina dropped Joe and Annie off and drove away. They came up the steps and into the house like the Feds on a narcotics raid.

"Henry!" Annie screeched, "Where are you, Henry? Look at all this stuff we got."

She spilled about three dozen little packages onto the sofa and stood back. "Smell me!" she commanded.

Henry had no choice. The kid must have tried on every perfume in the store. A cloud of fragrance surrounded her, spreading out in all directions. It hit you before she even got close to you, like a sort of sonic boom for noses.

"What did you get, kid?"

"Three pairs of shorts and six shirts—and some have satin, and some have lace—and perfume and a whole set of jewelry and some play makeup. This was the best shopping I ever did."

Joe had come into the room behind Henry. Now he put down an armful of packages.

"What did you get?" Henry asked, "a tubful of after-shave and some diamond watches?"

"No. I got a new glove."

"Who paid?"

"Me. And Aunt Wilhemina."

"You mean her five dollars, in your bank, and her whatever else it took today."

"Yuh. Well, I earned a dollar fifty last Sunday, don't forget—and anyway, I didn't ask to have that kid pour glue into my glove. That wasn't my fault."

"What else did you get?"

"Some shirts and shorts and things."

"What things?"

"Oh, a pair of running shoes and a new windbreaker . . . and some neat jogging shorts."

"But you don't run. The only running you do is to catch the school bus."

"Well, I'm going to start."

"Oh, yeah? When did you decide that?"

"Listen, Henry, you just lay off. I know what the trouble is with you. You're just jealous cause we

111

got all this stuff and you didn't. Well, you're the one who wouldn't go, so it's your own fault." Joe started to gather up his packages. "Come on, Annie. Let's get out of here."

"Sure—go on—get out of here. And take your junk with you. And when you're ready, you'll find your dinner in the oven, because I'm not going to hang around like your slave, waiting to serve you."

"Well, no one asked you to. No one ever asked you to," and Joe marched out of the room.

Annie, struggling to keep up, but dribbling packages behind her, looked after Joe and then back at Henry. "What's wrong, Henry?"

"Nothing you did, kid. You're OK. It's just that you've been bought and paid for—you and Joe."

"I still love you, Henry."

"I know that. Now take your stuff upstairs. I'll see you later. I'm going for a little walk."

It was after suppertime when Henry got back. He was tired, but he'd walked most of the anger out. Annie met him at the door, prancing around in the hall.

"Look, Henry! How do I look?" She was wearing makeup—put on, Henry thought, with a spoon. Around her neck and wrists, jewelry jingled and glittered. The perfume bombardment, surrounding her like a force field, seemed stronger, if anything. If she puts any more on,

Henry thought, it'll get so you can actually see it—like a blue cloud, following her everywhere.

He said, "Boy, Annie—you really are something."

"I'm wearing everything Aunt Wilhemina got me—except for the shorts and shirts."

"I could tell."

"Wait till I tell the kids at school."

"They're going to be impressed."

"And I got a card and a puzzle for Baby Ruth Carson. And Aunt Wilhemina helped me sign the card, and she had them wrap the puzzle. They're over there—on the hall table."

"Great."

She danced off, out to the porch, to show all her new things to Kitty.

Henry went in to watch television. No matter how aggravated he was, it always seemed to calm him down . . . and tonight, one of his favorite shows, *City Beat*, was on.

It was a suspenseful show, as usual, and during the program, Henry could hear approaching thunder outdoors, which made *City Beat* seem even more exciting. Talk about atmosphere!

Eight-thirty. *City Beat* came to a close with the last high-speed chase and a big crash scene. Henry sighed. Time to round up Annie. It sounded like she was still out on the porch, talking to Kitty.

"Time to go to bed, Annie."

"Can't I stay up just a little longer—till the thunder stops?"

"That thunder could go on all night."

"Please, Henry, Kitty's afraid of thunder."

Henry looked at the cat. It sat there beside Annie as if it had been carved out of ebony. If there was anything in the world that cat was afraid of, it wasn't letting on.

"Kitty can take care of himself." He took another look at the cat. "Why do you call him Kitty, anyway? He's got to weigh twenty pounds, at least. And Kitty sounds like a girl."

"He likes Kitty. When I call 'Kitty,' he comes."

"If I yelled, 'Sardines,' he'd come quicker."

"He would not. You just don't like him."

"Right. I just don't like him. So come on in and go to bed."

"I can't leave him out in a storm."

"Annie, for the last time, he can take care of himself. Besides, it's not storming. Now move it!"

Annie gave Kitty one long, lingering hug and went indoors silently.

Henry gave her plenty of time to get ready for bed and calm down, and then he went up to say good-night and tell her, again, not to worry about the cat.

She was lying there with her night-light on and her eyes shut. They were shut so tight there were

114

wrinkles above her nose and her eyebrows came down low over her eyelids. No one slept like that! But when Henry said, "Annie?" she didn't answer.

He went out, closing the door behind him a little louder than necessary, and feeling a little hurt.

He decided to turn in early himself. What a day! He climbed the attic stairs hoping that his mother would say something to make him feel better.

"Ma."

"Hello, Henry. I missed you at dinner."

"Yuh. Well, I wasn't hungry."

"So I gathered."

"You saw what Aunt Wilhemina got Joe and Annie?"

His mother grinned. "Yes, I saw."

"Ma—Annie looks like a midget hooker, and she jingles like a belly dancer . . . and she smells like a . . ."

"Henry!"

"Well, she does. You know darned well that you'd never have picked out all that junk, if you'd been there."

"I know. But it gives Aunt Wilhemina pleasure to indulge Annie . . . and she did pay for all the extras herself."

"It didn't exactly make either of them unhappy to be indulged, either."

"Henry—you could have gone, too."

"Sure—I could have gone—and if I had, they would still have brought home perfume and baseball gloves, and she would have gotten me some book on How To Improve Your Mind, or maybe some galoshes, on sale."

"Do I detect just a touch of self-pity here?"

Henry snorted.

"I understand Joe is going to take up running."

Henry said, "If he gets so he can run a mile in under fifteen minutes, I'll buy his next pair of running shoes myself. As it is, he can just barely make it around the bases in time. The best thing he does is eat."

"Well, maybe Aunt Wilhemina had that in mind. Maybe, if we can all encourage Joe to do a little running, he'll pick up some speed and lose a little weight."

"That's not why she got him all that stuff, Ma—she's trying to buy her way in here."

"Henry, I am still running this family. Remember that."

There was an awkward pause, and then Henry pointed to her work and asked, "How's it coming?"

"It's coming better. I got a lot done, today. But there's still no way that I can have everything the way I want it in time."

"I'm sorry, Ma."

"So am I. Every so often today, I thought maybe

I'd be able to get it all whipped into shape in time, but I was just kidding myself. I'm getting more and more tired and going slower all the time—and time is what I haven't got."

"Well, you gave it a good try. No one could have tried harder."

"Sometimes I think maybe I could have tried harder."

"Ma, you only took time out to eat and sleep. How could anyone do more than that?"

She nodded. Suddenly, she laid her head down on the table.

Henry said, "I wish you'd never seen that ad! You've been knocking yourself out for two lousy weeks—and now what? Nothing!"

She sat up again. "No. Not for nothing. It was right to at least try, wasn't it? It's changed me. It's brought out a side of me I'd let die for all these years. That's worth something."

"What is it worth? If you don't get the job, and you end up unhappy like this—what's it all been for?"

She didn't answer.

"I wish you'd never seen the ad," he repeated and stumped downstairs. But at the foot of the stairs, he turned and yelled up, "Good night, Ma. I love you."

"Good night, Henry. I love you, too."

Chapter Sixteen

Monday   June 14

HE HAD JUST GOTTEN TO SLEEP when the storm broke and woke him up. The lightning began to flicker almost continuously, and the thunder rolled back and forth above the house till it wasn't frightening—just irritating. Henry couldn't take it any longer. He got up, swearing, and stumped downstairs in the dark.

When he threw open the front door, the cat was out there—waiting for him. Henry had known he would be. Oh, he was sure of himself, that one. He was sitting on the welcome mat. Naturally. But the rain, drumming on the porch steps and railings, was throwing a fine mist over him, and his smooth, glossy coat was now patchy with dampness. His tail twitched uncomfortably on the wet mat. He looked up and meowed. Just once.

"OK. Come in." Henry opened the screen door, and the cat slipped silently inside.

"And stay downstairs," Henry said.

He shut the front door and headed back upstairs, swinging wide around the cat as he passed.

He shut his door, just in case, and crawled back

into bed. You'd think a cat like that would have been able to find a dry place to stay. Dumb cat! Waiting out there on the porch all night. What if no one had come? What then?

He fell asleep almost immediately.

Tuesday morning was bright and cool. Henry got up feeling fine. He opened his door cautiously—no cat. He went down the stairs two at a time—no cat. He jogged into the kitchen—no cat! But his mother had already been and gone. Her dishes were rinsed and stacked in the sink. Well, it was still a great morning—and his mother had probably put the cat out.

He set out the breakfast things and started on making the lunches. Everything was going well, till he tried to open the new package of luncheon meat. It said OPEN HERE, and he tried. He tried here, and there, and there, and there. He tried ripping it open with his teeth and sawing at it with a table knife. He tried skewering it with a fork— and ran one of the tines into his finger, which meant, he concluded sadly, that his finger was made of less durable material than the package. That made him feel a little guilty—as if he was criticizing God, or something. He got out his mother's serrated carving knife, which was kept in a cardboard sheath, it was so sharp, and started to saw away.

The knife was certainly sharp. It cut through the package and into Henry's thumb, with almost no effort. Henry stood there, looking at his thumb for a minute, in amazement. There was the cut—and it was a big one, all right—but it wasn't even bleeding.

Then, the bleeding started. And he had to race upstairs for a bandage, holding his thumb tightly in a dish towel, to keep from staining the rugs. He passed Joe and Annie coming downstairs for breakfast, on his way up, but he felt that speed was more important than sociability (the dish towel was already turning red in its thickest part) so he just whizzed right on past.

He missed the school bus, of course. But, after losing all that blood, he did not think it was fair to expect him to walk to school, too—so he broke one of his own ironclad rules and interrupted his mother and asked her to drive him to school.

They passed the bathroom going downstairs. "Good Lord, Henry!"

"I'll clean it all up later, Ma," he said modestly, feeling some pride that he was still bravely carrying on—and quite pleased that she had noticed the mess in the bathroom.

She was quiet as she drove to the school, except for an occasional remark to the effect that no job was worth it—and that he could have bled to death—and that if her appointment with Mr. Bennett weren't tomorrow, anyway, she'd give the whole thing up.

Henry's warm glow lasted until halfway through his first class, when he remembered that he hadn't eaten any breakfast, he hadn't brought any lunch, and neither, as far as he knew, had Joe and Annie. All he'd brought, picked up as he went through the hall, were Baby Ruth Carson's card and puzzle. He went through his pockets. No money. Naturally. He'd have to borrow from Charley Weideberg, again. Boy! She was right. No job was worth it.

The minute school got out, Henry headed down the street towards the hospital. If he moved fast, he could deliver Annie's stuff to Baby Ruth Carson and get back to the school yard in time to at least watch some softball before the late bus left.

He had never been in a hospital before—except, of course, for the Emergency Room downstairs, which he and Joe had visited fairly frequently over the years. But he had no trouble finding the big directory in the lobby, and when he saw PEDIAT-RICS–3 he knew that meant they kept the little kids up on the third floor. The elevator carried him silently up to the third floor and let him out. No problem.

He looked around. A hospital was really just like a big hotel. Without carpets.

He stepped up to the desk opposite the elevators and, trying to look as tall and sound as mature as possible, he asked what room Carson was in.

The nurse didn't even look up. "All the way down the hall on your left, then turn right. Third door on your right."

He was making the turn to the right when someone called him by name. "Henry! Henry Walker!"

He stopped and turned around cautiously. He didn't think he was known in this place . . . outside of the Emergency Room. What had he done wrong already?

It was just Dr. Temple—their family doctor. He hurried down the hall towards Henry . . . a short, chubby man who looked as if he was smiling even when he was dozing off in church.

"Henry, my boy! I thought it was you . . . couldn't miss that red hair. Who's sick? Not Joe or Annie . . . and it wouldn't be your delightful mother—on this floor."

"No. Just a kid we know—Carson."

The doctor stopped walking along beside Henry. "Baby Ruth Carson? You're visiting her? Now that's very nice. Yes."

Henry shrugged. He had been so unwilling to

make this visit, he didn't feel right accepting any compliments on doing it.

"She needs company. Oh, yes. Been no one to see her since Sunday morning. And she wasn't really alert then."

"No one?"

"No one," Dr. Temple said firmly. "Of course, they all came for the operation—and I'm not saying that's not important, mind you . . . to be there, when the child comes out of the anesthesia. But, since then . . ." He shook his head. "Of course, with seven boys and three girls—all of them hell on wheels, mind you—Mrs. Carson has her hands full. And Mr. Carson has his own problems, but even so. And, if they're running true to form, they won't be back till it's time to take her home. They call and check with the head nurse— but, what with no car . . . and other things I can't go into . . . no one ever seems to get down here." He shook his head. "I tell you, my boy, I worry about little ones like that . . . quiet and withdrawn. She spends a lot of time just looking out the window at nothing. Now, you know that's not normal, for that age."

"That's just Baby Ruth, Dr. Temple. I wouldn't worry."

"Well, I do worry. People need to feel that someone cares. Particularly little people."

"Oh."

"Don't say it like that, Henry. Don't ever under-estimate caring. I don't. No, sir. There's just so much any of us doctors can do, and then it's up to the patient. You see what I mean? And if the patient gets to feeling that no one else gives a damn . . . it can be an uphill fight to bring them through the common cold. Yes, sir." He turned toward Henry and shook a finger at him. "Don't you know your Bible, boy? 'A merry heart doeth good like a medicine. . . .' Proverbs . . . that goes way back."

Henry nodded obediently. Boy, Dr. Temple was really wound up today.

To his astonishment, Dr. Temple suddenly grabbed him by the elbow, turned him around, and steered him back down the long hall. "I want to show you something, Henry . . . my idea to begin with. It's worked like a charm, too—been going on for five years, now. My pet project." He trotted past the main desk and turned, without any warning, into a door labeled NURSERY.

"Look in there—on your left."

Henry peered through the plate glass. There were four rockers and four little tables, in a small room on his left. Three of the rockers were occupied by women wearing white caps, masks, and hospital uniforms. They were rocking away, and they were holding little blanket-rolled babies.

"That's my Granny Squad. They give the babies

a lot of holding and rocking and baby talk . . . the little ones who have to stay here, for some reason, when their mothers go home—or the babies whose mothers aren't quite up to taking care of them. The women work with the older children, too. I guess they rock away miles, every day. And they take book carts around and read to the ones like Baby Ruth. Volunteers, mind you. No pay."

"How about that."

Dr. Temple headed back towards the main desk. "Babies can die from not enough holding and talking and love, you know. Oh yes. First, they begin to withdraw a little—maybe they stop eating and playing. You could say they lose interest. They sort of retreat into their own little shell and just lie there, waiting. They fade right in front of your eyes—and before long, some disease or other gets them . . . something they should have been able to throw off just like that!" He snapped his stubby fingers high in the air. "It's called 'failure to thrive,' by some people"—he pounded his right fist into the palm of his left hand—"but I call it a crime."

"They died? Really died?"

"Died! But not here. Not as long as we stay alert and have our little Granny Squad." He turned toward the stairs. "Have a nice visit, my boy," and was gone.

Henry had planned to spend maybe thirty seconds, at the most, in Baby Ruth's room, but after his tour with Dr. Temple, he didn't dare do that. Then, if the kid died from whatever cause, he'd feel that if he'd stayed longer, it wouldn't have happened.

She was lying in the bed, looking out the window. Well, Dr. Temple had called that shot. She looked skinny and pale. Henry coughed. Her head snapped around, and her eyes came to life.

"I brought you some things from Annie. She couldn't come. She's too young."

She nodded.

He placed the card and the puzzle directly on her bed, beside her hand.

"I can stay for a little while—till it's time to catch the late bus. You want me to read to you or something?"

There was a long pause. Then, very slightly, she nodded.

"OK. You got anything to read in here?"

She shook her head, "No."

"I'll be right back."

The nurse at the main desk said, "The book cart will be around at five."

"That's too late. I need something to read to a little kid, now."

"All I've got is one of my own personal magazines."

"I'll bring it back."

127

She bent down and rummaged around under the counter. She came up again with *Family Journal.* "I don't know if this is what you had in mind."

"It'll do. Thanks."

Henry began with what turned out to be a really sickening love story—but Baby Ruth seemed to be paying close attention, so he kept on going to the end. When he finished, he looked at her and made a face, expressing, he hoped, extreme disgust. She nodded and pantomimed throwing up.

He went on to a story for children. It was pretty sickening, too. At the end, he said, "Boy!" She nodded and made a face indicating a very low opinion of the story.

He kept on going, straight through a group of strawberry recipes. The pictures were nice. Baby Ruth said, "I'm not real hungry yet," and pointed in the general direction of where her appendix used to be.

He plowed through the poetry page—three of them weren't too bad—and an article on children's television viewing habits, which he felt was way off base. Baby Ruth said, "No one's going to tell me how much television to watch."

Henry nodded. It was his guess that no one told Baby Ruth anything.

His time was up. "I've got to go. I hope you feel better."

She said, "I'll look at this stuff later—when you're gone."

"OK."

"Tell Annie thanks."

"I will. Good-bye."

She stirred and struggled to sit up higher. "When I get home, I'll make you another cookie."

Henry said, "Well, make it soon—because I *need* another one, to balance my mantel."

She smiled.

Henry left. Dr. Temple would be proud of him. Heck, he was proud of him. And feeling good.

The house was awfully quiet when he got home. He found Joe in the kitchen, painting. Joe's tongue was stuck out one corner of his mouth and curled up at the end, he was concentrating so hard.

"Hey, Joe. How's it coming?"

"OK."

"Where's Annie? I just saw Baby Ruth."

"I don't know. She had something to eat—and took off." Joe looked up. "You ought to do something about that kid. She must have taken three, maybe four, sandwiches. If she keeps on eating like that . . ."

"What did you two do for lunch?"

"Borrowed," and Joe went back to his work.

Henry took a couple of bananas and wandered

off up to his room. As he passed Annie's room, something struck him as not right. He backed up and looked in again.

All her drawers were open—every single one—and her closet door was wide open, too. Well—maybe the kid had been looking for something, in a hurry. And everything on her mantel was gone—all of her favorite things . . . her white china cat, her stuffed calico cat, her prism, and a vase of plastic flowers that he'd won for her once at a carnival. That was strange.

He walked into the room and stood there, conscious of a growing, clutching uneasiness. Then, he bent down against his will and looked under her bed. Her little plaid overnight bag was gone.

Chapter Seventeen

Tuesday June 15

HE STRAIGHTENED UP. Annie was gone. Kitty! She'd never go without Kitty! He ran downstairs and grabbed a can of tuna. He opened it and flipped the contents out onto a plate. Then, he went out into the backyard. Joe put down his brush and followed him.

"What are you doing?"

"Looking for Kitty."

"Really, what are you doing?"

"I'm really looking for Kitty. Call him, will you? Go around front. Here—take some tuna. He'll smell it."

"I don't need any tuna. He'll come out if I call," and Joe walked off towards the front of the house.

"Kitty? Kitty! Here, Kitty."

Henry hated Kitty as a cat's name. At least give the animal a decent name—like Tex, or Dolly. Now, however, he would have used any name known to man, if only the big, black cat would come to it. But he didn't.

He met Joe coming around the corner of the house.

Joe said, "Why are we looking for Kitty?"

"Because I think Annie's gone—and she wouldn't go without taking Kitty."

"Right. So why aren't we calling, 'Annie!'—if she's really the one we want. I mean—Kitty's a nice cat, and all that, but . . ."

"OK. OK. You're right. Yell for Annie."

Henry allowed himself five more minutes for calling the cat and Annie. After that, he'd have to alert his mother. There were maybe three hours left before it got dark.

The attic stairs had never seemed so long, or so steep.

"Ma, I think Annie's left."

"How do you mean, Henry?"

"Run away."

His mother stood up, scattering brushes and paper onto the floor. "When?"

"Probably right after school. I just now found out."

"How can you be sure? She's probably just outdoors, playing."

"No. Kitty's gone, and Annie's plaid bag is gone, and she took everything off her mantel. And Joe complained about her taking three or four sandwiches as a snack. I didn't think anything about that, at the time . . . but now . . ."

His mother was already halfway down the attic stairs.

She went through Annie's things. "Her coat is missing, and her Peanuts sweat shirt, and her slicker. She wouldn't have worn those things today, would she? No. So—she took them for warmth, at night. Call the neighbors, Henry . . . all up and down the street, and all of Annie's friends. Tell them we want her home for some reason. Joe, you come with me in the car, and we'll drive around for a while, looking. And Henry— keep calling. Call anyone who might have seen her or talked to her."

"Right."

Half an hour later, the car pulled into the driveway. Henry ran out the front door. Joe and his mother got out.

"I called everyone, Ma—for miles. No one has seen her."

"Well, that settles it. We'll have to call the police. They'll want a picture. Joe—you get our album—it's in my room. Henry, just in case, you go around the yard looking everywhere she might hide. Then, open every closet door. Look in the basement. And then, you go over to the Carson place, and call to her in the woods around their house. Maybe she left, but didn't go too far. She's only a little girl." His mother's voice broke for a moment, but she kept on going. "So, maybe she stayed close to home but is afraid to come out, or fell asleep."

The police came right away. They took the pictures Ma and Joe had picked out of the album. They asked a lot of questions. They went all through the house and the yard. They promised to call as soon as they'd found her.

Then, Henry's mother went out in the car again—up one street and down the next. Joe said he'd stay by the phone, for calls coming in. Henry got out his big flashlight and started searching again, on foot. He imagined a giant spiral, with his house at its center, and he started walking out the spiral in circles, each one a little larger than the last. He went across backyards, over stone walls, through hedges. He jumped little creeks, crossed streets where everyone was driving too fast, and stepped over flower beds. He called, "Annie!" till he was hoarse.

By now, it was really dark. He stopped walking and sat down on a curb. He was so tired, he could have rolled over right there and gone to sleep on the sidewalk, if he'd known Annie was safe. Maybe she'd been found already. Maybe he should go home and check with Joe. He headed back towards the house.

The minute he saw Joe, he knew Annie was still lost.

"Nothing?"

"Nothing. People have called—to see if she was found. Aunt Wilhemina called, too."

"What'd you tell her?" Henry asked wearily.

"Just what happened."

"Oh, boy. When did she call?"

"About half an hour ago."

"Well, she should be here any minute." Henry sat down on the front stairs, and leaned up against the wall. Across the step from him was the beginning of a new pile of Annie's things—her red jump rope, of course, a doll, a box containing some puzzle pieces, and a couple of picture books—all waiting to go upstairs someday. He felt like crying when he saw it. If Joe hadn't been there, maybe he would have.

He heard car brakes screeching and knew that Aunt Wilhemina had arrived. When something big was happening, she always drove as if she were leading the attack. He wanted to just float out the back door and disappear, but he didn't.

"Boys! Any news?"

Joe said, "No."

"How did this happen? Where is your mother?"

Joe said, "Ma's out, driving around."

Henry said, "Annie just took off."

"Why, for heaven's sake? Did someone say something to her? Was she being punished for something?"

Henry said, "No one knows, Aunt Wilhemina. She didn't tell us. She didn't leave a note or anything."

"Well, there certainly must have been some reason."

Joe said, "She was awfully upset about that cat, Henry."

"What happened to the cat?" Aunt Wilhemina demanded.

"Nothing happened to the cat. I guess Joe means when I made her leave the cat out at night."

"Yuh. With the storm and all," Joe said. "And some little kid on the bus was saying how her family had taken a bunch of kittens to the pound, and what they do to them if no one wants them . . . and maybe Annie thought we'd do that to Kitty."

"Why would she think a thing like that?" Aunt Wilhemina demanded, looking at Henry.

"I never said I'd do that!" he shouted. "I never would."

Joe said, "Who knows what a little kid will think, Aunt Wilhemina? They all go around crazy half the time, anyway. And there were other things—like this morning, no lunches, and no nickel for milk, and no one else around but her and me . . . and Baby Ruth, her best friend, being so sick. . . . She was worried about Baby Ruth. I think maybe she got to feeling sorry for herself. She makes a big deal out of everything, when she gets to feeling sorry for herself."

Henry said, "I let that cat in last night, you know."

Joe's eyebrows went up. "I didn't know that."

Aunt Wilhemina said, "Well, this is what comes of lack of supervision. Many's the time I have offered to come here and help—but No! It wasn't necessary. Well—this just shows that it was necessary. If I had been here, the cat"—and she gave Henry a stern, meaningful stare—"would have been in its rightful place—at Annie's side . . . and lunches would have been provided."

For one wild, crazy moment, Henry had an irresistible urge to ask her how she would have healed Baby Ruth, but he put a lid on it.

Joe said, "Henry always gave us lunches before."

Henry hated to have to explain or justify anything to Aunt Wilhemina, but this was a bad situation. "I cut my hand this morning." He held up his bandaged thumb. "It was bleeding all over everything. I had to go upstairs to bandage it."

She seized on this triumphantly. Her eyes actually seemed to glitter behind her glasses. "You see? You see? This family is going to the dogs. I knew Ellen was taking on too much. I warned her. But she wouldn't listen. Now look where it's all led to. . . ."

Henry stood up. "We were doing fine. I was doing OK. I made a mistake about the cat—but I was doing my best. Ma and I had everything under control."

"And where is your sister, tonight?" she demanded.

"I'm going!" He picked up his flashlight. "Turn all the lights on, Joe—if they find Annie. I'll know to quit looking, if I see the house lit up. Otherwise, I would have to come in to check."

"Right."

He sat down outside in the dark. Now, he had time to think. He and Ma and Joe knew Annie better than anybody. They should be able to figure where she'd go. If she took all that heavy clothing, she meant to stay out all night. But a little kid like Annie wouldn't just lie down in an open field. She'd try to find a corner—a closed-in spot—where she would feel protected. And she'd want to keep Kitty with her, for company, if she could.

That last point kept coming back to him. Was there any way she could be sure that the cat would stay with her? What would keep a cat from leaving? A leash. But, as far as he knew, Annie didn't have a leash for Kitty. What about water? Cats didn't like to go through water.

Water. Creeks. There were lots of creeks around, and some had little islands jutting up in midstream.

An island would feel good to a little kid. It would feel safe. And, on an island, she'd know that if she woke up at night, Kitty would still be there.

If he were a little kid, he'd pick a small island—with trees on it—and it would have to be in a small creek, so he could wade across to it. Annie wasn't a good swimmer, and she had all that stuff, plus the cat, to take with her.

So—a small island, in a small creek. He thought it over and selected three possibilities. One was a couple of miles away. Too far. She'd never make it on her own, carrying a twenty-pound cat. The second was a lot closer, but the creek around it was a tidal creek, which meant that sometimes it was very deep and very fast. Henry felt a fresh wave of fear flash over him. He hoped she hadn't tried for that one. In his mind's eye, just for a second—till he blotted it out—he saw Annie struggling in the current, and going under. He got up and started jogging in the direction of the third possibility.

The creek—Willow Creek—was about a mile away. There were a couple of little islands in it—covered with willow trees and scrub. Two of them were so tiny and flat that they disappeared under water for a while every spring—but the third was a real, high and dry little island. And, if she chose her footing carefully, she could wade across.

He could hear the creek now . . . gurgling and bubbling to itself in the darkness. He worked his way up the bank, looking for the cut that went down to the water's edge. Here it was—a slash in the undergrowth . . . a little chute straight down to the water.

He slid down and stood up again at the water's edge. The water was black in the beam from his flashlight. The island looked bigger and farther away than he remembered it. He stood there for a minute, trying to gather up enough courage to step out into the creek.

"Annie?"

No answer.

"Annie?"

Nothing. He strained to listen above the sibilant river noises. Annie was a deep sleeper. She might be out there and just not hearing him.

"Kitty!" He felt foolish, standing there in the dark, calling for a cat instead of his sister—but the cat was probably a lighter sleeper. What counted now was results. "Kitty!"

He heard it—unmistakably—an answering meow. Then, two tiny globes of amber appeared in the brush across the water—the cat's eyes, reflecting his flashlight beam. And if Kitty was out there, Annie was out there.

He plunged recklessly into the water—not caring how deep it was—and not picking his steps at all. He plowed across the creek, splashing, slipping, falling—leaving a wake of white bubbles floating downstream on the black water behind him. Now, he was coming up into shallower water—and now, he was right in amongst the willows. Kitty meowed at him and retreated through the brush. Henry followed him, not daring to lose sight of him. He led Henry right to Annie. She was curled up at the base of a tremendous willow. Her head rested on her little plaid bag, and her yellow slicker gleamed in the light.

"Annie! You crazy kid, wake up! You had us all scared to death."

Annie scrambled to her feet, shielding her eyes from Henry's light. "Henry? Is that you?"

"Damn right it is. Do you know how scared I've been? Everyone's out looking for you. . . ." He grabbed her and hugged her.

She started to snuffle. "Is Ma mad at me?"

"Not yet. Worried sick, maybe." He bent down and picked up her bag. "We're going home, now. Can you carry that cat?"

"I think so. I brought him over this afternoon."

"OK. Let's get going."

It was rough, going back. Annie kept slipping, and once she fell, and the cat, frantic at falling and being dipped into the cold water, scratched her. She started to cry.

Henry could just see her six years from now, no longer able to enjoy Kitty, but feeling sick every time a cat came near her—like him. "Here—give me that cat, and you hold on to my belt, see—so you won't fall. Just take it easy."

Annie handed him the cat. Henry could feel it resisting, but he set his jaw, prepared for the worst, and took it into the angle of his free arm. It clawed its way up to his shoulder and travelled the rest of the way across the creek around his neck. It was funny, but clinging to him like that, curled around his shoulders, wet and miserable and frightened, Kitty didn't feel like he weighed twenty pounds, after all. He felt kind of light and pretty small, actually. He was just a small, wet, scared animal—who needed to be held up above the cold black waters.

"Are you all right, Henry?"

"Yes. Except for this cat's tail in my mouth."

"He's a very clean cat, Henry."

"Terrific. That takes a load off my mind."

They paused to rest and shift their burdens on the shore. It was decided that Annie would take the flashlight and go ahead, while Henry would take the bag in one hand and the cat, who had calmed down, in the other arm, and follow.

In twenty minutes, they could see the house. Aunt Wilhemina's car was still there, and Henry's mother's car was there.

In another five minutes, they were home. Henry sank down on the porch steps and let Kitty and Annie go the rest of the way on their own. If he never moved again, it would be too soon.

The police were called and told about Annie's safe return, and they returned the pictures by squad car. Aunt Wilhemina was invited to come back soon and eased out. Joe was sent to bed, and Annie was tubbed and tucked in. Henry sat at the dining room table. He was terribly tired, but his mind kept buzzing around like a hornet against an attic window.

"I'm sorry about losing Annie, Ma."

"But you found her. And it's not so unusual, Henry—children running away. It seems to me that both you and Joe ran away for an hour or so, when you were little. You've done a marvelous job, the last two weeks. I'm just sorry it had to end like this." She reached over and squeezed his hand.

"I was wrong about the cat—and I made a lot of other mistakes, too."

"No one's perfect." She grinned and looked up at the wall clock. "Hey—it seems to me we've had this conversation, before."

"Yuh. We were talking about Aunt Wilhemina, two weeks ago."

"Yes, I remember." She stood up. "Time for bed. Take the photo album up with you, won't you, dear?" She slipped the pictures they'd given the police back into the album, and a big snapshot fell out on the floor. Henry bent down and picked it up. It was of Aunt Wilhemina and Ma and Henry's father, and some little kid all bundled up in a blanket. Aunt Wilhemina was the one in the middle, holding the baby. It was strange to see her like that—holding it so carefully, as if it were made of diamonds and china. Her big hands were just sort of wrapped around the baby, like she was guarding it.

"Who's the kid?"

"You. You were about three months old, there. Aunt Wilhemina was so thrilled when you were born." She took the picture from him. "I've always planned to have this picture enlarged and framed. I think I'll really do it now."

Henry said, "I was so little."

"Yes. You were. And now, you're almost a man." She sounded sad—as if she were telling him someone had died—and that made Henry feel guilty.

He stood up again. "Good night, Ma."

"Good night, dear."

He sat on the edge of his bed. Maybe Aunt Wilhemina was right. Maybe Joe and Annie did need someone else, and maybe he wasn't enough. He'd never been so scared in his life, as when he realized that Annie had run off. It wouldn't have happened if Aunt Wilhemina had been here. He rocked back and forth on the edge of his bed, struggling to sort things out in his mind.

Either his mother would get this great job, or she wouldn't. If she did, it would mean she could only be their part-time mother, and so maybe that would mean Aunt Wilhemina, after all. If she didn't, it might mean moving—or Aunt Wilhemina, because of the money.

If he'd been able to do a better job these past two weeks . . . If he'd been able to handle Kitty without practically passing out . . . If he'd gotten along better somehow with Joe and Annie . . .

The only thing left to do was to figure out what was best for everybody—and just sort of go along with it. If that meant having Aunt Wilhemina move in, then he'd just have to learn to keep his mouth shut, till he was big enough to be on his own. Ma was right. He was almost a man. But what had gone wrong between him and Aunt Wilhemina? . . . Between her holding him like that and giving him old bars of soap. What had gone wrong?

Chapter Eighteen

Wednesday   June 16

HIS MOTHER was finishing her coffee in the kitchen when he came down. She looked grim.

"Are you ready?" he asked.

"No. But we gave it a good try, didn't we?"

"We sure did. Can I see the portfolio, now?"

She nodded.

He opened it. The pictures were in pen and ink, and watercolors. A unicorn, bearing a laughing group of children, danced down a starry sky. You could almost feel the stars tingling as the children brushed past. A small, tired boy leaned up against his grandmother, as they sat on an old wooden porch. It was a hot summer's day, and a kind of lazy warmth radiated up from the page. A fox trip-trotted across a meadow full of flowers, in the early morning. They were beautiful pictures. Really beautiful. Every one of them—and there were ten in all—was better than Henry would have believed possible. It was weird—looking at his mother's pictures—as if she were showing him a fourth child, all her own, that she'd kept hidden somewhere all these years. He felt a jealousy rise in him—that she had this thing she did so well and loved to do so much—and it was a thing that he had no part in.

He looked up. His mother had been watching him, and she turned away as if she was embarrassed to be caught watching him.

"Ma—these are great."

She busied herself with fastening up the portfolio. "You really like them?"

"I do."

"Thank you, Henry. I was afraid you might not like them." She was ready to go, but she hovered, still—nervous and fluttering.

"I don't care what happens, Ma—I hope you get the job." And he felt calm inside, at last. He meant it. It was all settled. She should get the job. She deserved it.

"I hope so, too—except that it raises so many questions."

"Yuh. Well, he's going to hire you. I know it."

The day went by so slowly, Henry wanted to throw something, or just yell, from sheer tension. Win or lose, he had to have some definite answers soon, or he would bust. His mother was home when he walked in. He could smell her perfume. She burst through the back hall door as he came into the front hall. She came running toward him.

"I got it!"

"I knew you would, Ma," and he hugged her hard. Joe and Annie, having finally caught up with him, joined the group. There was a lot of hugging and kissing and a little crying—the regular "excited family" routine.

Then Joe and Annie disentangled themselves and headed for the kitchen.

Henry said, "What'll we do, now, Ma?"

She smiled mysteriously. "Well, Mr. Bennett and I discussed my assignments for the next few months, and I think . . ."

She paused until Henry said, "Yes?"

". . . I think that with a little help from my friends, I can do it—without calling in the reserves."

"You mean—just by ourselves?" Henry had to be sure. "In spite of Annie's running away?"

"Yes. There's no reason why I can't handle my work during the school day—and why we can't all manage the rest on our own. I told you those first two weeks, when I was making up for years of lost time, would be the worst."

"No Aunt Wilhemina?" Henry sat down. "No moving?"

"No. But we'll have to have her over, now and then—for dinner. We'll have something special, like Heads Up Veal."

Henry grinned.

"And Henry, do try harder to understand her, dear. Please. For me. Because she means well. She's just full of love that hasn't got an outlet. No one needs her anymore. She wants to take care of someone, but people grow up—and then they don't want to be taken care of. Think back over these past two weeks, Henry. In spite of the work and the worry and the aggravation—wasn't it kind of nice to be indispensable? Won't you miss that, just a little?"

Henry nodded.

"That's why she can't seem to stop meddling. It's awful, Henry, not to be needed at all. Every time I see her, or think about her, I feel sad."

Henry felt an idea stirring in the back of his mind. "You said she was real glad when I was born. She likes babies?"

"She loves them! She adores them! She's a different person when she's holding a baby."

"And she needs to be needed?"

"Desperately."

In his mind's eye, Henry could see someone filling that fourth rocker in the hospital nursery. He smiled. "Ma, have you ever heard of a group called the Granny Squad?"

ABOUT THE AUTHOR

ALISON SMITH is the author of *Reserved for Mark Anthony Crowder,* which won the International Reading Association's Children's Book Award in 1979. She and her family live in Harmony, Rhode Island.

ABOUT THE ILLUSTRATOR

AMY ROWEN illustrated *Casey and the Great Idea* by Joan Lowery Nixon and *Bus Ride* by Marilyn Sachs. She lives in New York City.

WANT TO READ THE MOST EXCITING BOOKS AROUND?
CHOOSE CHOOSE YOUR OWN ADVENTURE®

Everybody loves CHOOSE YOUR OWN ADVENTURE® books because the stories are about you. Each book is loaded with choices that only you can make. Instead of reading from the first page to the last page, you read until you come to your first choice. Then, depending on your decision, you turn to a new page to see what happens next. And you can keep reading and rereading CHOOSE YOUR OWN ADVENTURE® books because every choice leads to a new adventure and there are lots of different ways for the story to end.

Buy these great CHOOSE YOUR OWN ADVENTURE® books, available wherever Bantam Skylark books are sold or use the handy coupon below for ordering: